Published by DREAMSPINNER PRESS   http://www.dreamspinnerpress.com

Published by DREAMSPINNER PRESS
http://www.dreamspinnerpress.com

Readers Love Andrew Grey

A Heart Without Borders

"I felt like I was right there with the characters, feeling the heat, the desperation and the total devastation right along with them. There is no doubt in my mind that this book will stay with me for a long time."

—The Novel Approach

"In true Andrew Grey fashion, this book delivers not only a romance but a powerful lesson on the courage, hope and optimism of people in a country devastated by disaster and poverty."

—Hearts on Fire Reviews

Stranded

"A great story of how time passes and people allow their relationship to settle into routine and they lose their appreciation for their partner. This doesn't mean that they are no longer deeply in love, sometimes they just need a reminder."

—Gay List Book Reviews

"*Stranded* is an amazing combination between an intense thriller-like stalker story, a sizzling romance, and a character study which, through tension and drama, brings out the worst and the best in both main characters."

—Rainbow Book Reviews

A Daring Ride

"All the things we've come to love from Grey are there in the print. An emotional, engrossing, and sexy ride is what's in store with this latest work from one of the best authors in the genre."

—MM Good Book Reviews

"I quickly got sucked in by the story and the characters. There really is so much substance in the plot and the people… he doesn't need a lot of extra language to pull you in."

—Mrs. Condit & Friends Read Books

Readers Love Andrew Grey

An Isolated Range

"Mr. Grey delivers a highly emotional story that captures the reader's heart in one fell swoop. This is an author who is dedicated to his series, stories and characters. With each range story, you always find yourself drawn in, breathless until the very last page is read."

—Dawn's Reading Nook

"Andrew Grey's Range series just gets stronger with each new book and *An Isolated Range* is perhaps the most amazing addition yet."

—Scattered Thoughts and Rogue Words

"*An Isolated Range* is a story not of human triumphs but also of sadness and death. This is an author who balances both so well that the reader is left speechless after that last page is read."

—Love Romances and More

The Fight Within

"I loved this book, these characters, and this story. Get it today. Read. Understand and through understanding, enjoy."

—Mrs. Condit & Friends Read Books

"This is a story that is rich in detail, delving into the Native American culture and also sharing the suffering that the Native American's still face today."

—MM Good Book Reviews

"This was a very powerful read."

—Live your Life, Buy the Book

CROSSING DIVIDES

ANDREW GREY

Dreamspinner Press

Published by
Dreamspinner Press
5032 Capital Circle SW
Suite 2, PMB# 279
Tallahassee, FL 32305-7886
USA
http://www.dreamspinnerpress.com/

Crossing Divides
© 2013 Andrew Grey.

Cover Art
© 2013 L.C. Chase.
http://www.lcchase.com
Cover content is for illustrative purposes only and any person depicted on the cover is a model.

ISBN: 978-1-62798-326-6
Digital ISBN: 978-1-62798-327-3

Printed in the United States of America
First Edition
December 2013

To Dominic, for always believing in me.

CHAPTER
ONE

"WHY IN the hell did I ever agree to do this?" Carter Hopkins asked himself. He was over thirty and should know better. He lifted his head, and the freedom fighter next to him pushed it back down.

"Don't lift that thing unless you want to lose it," Jalal growled in a heavy accent and then added words in Arabic that Carter couldn't understand, but he got the gist of it. It most likely centered on something about the stupid American, only put in a much more *colorful* way. Rifle chatter near Carter's head made him hug the ground, trying to figure out how he could dig the depression they had jumped into deeper.

A bullet zinged over his head, and Carter swore under his breath. "I'm going to kill my fucking editor when I get back."

"I'm going to kill him too," Jalal gritted out. "Maybe we do it together." Then his automatic rifle spat again. Carter stayed where he was, praying silently that the band of men he was with could hold their position. First, because this was an impressive group of men fighting for what they saw as the possibility of a brighter future for themselves and their children, and second because if they couldn't hold their ground, it appeared they'd be overrun, and Carter really wasn't looking to be held and questioned in a Syrian government prison.

Carter jumped when rifle fire began again, this time coming at them in earnest. The men around him let out a cry that made Carter shiver. Fuck, this was annoying. He'd been to war zones before—Iraq, Afghanistan—but this wasn't war; it was chaos with bombs and bullets. One day the rebels would take a position, the government would take it back the following day, and then the men he was with would retake the same ground the following day. The whistle of a shell overhead caught his attention. He tried to follow the sound, but it got mixed in with the million other noises assaulting his hearing and he lost track of it. Carter felt the explosion vibrate through the ground, followed by the cries of men. They were far enough away that he knew it wasn't their men.

All the men around him suddenly came to their feet, yelling and screaming as they rushed away. "Stay here," Jalal commanded, and Carter nodded. Jalal jumped out of the trench and raced away. Carter stayed right where he was and waited. More fire erupted, farther away, and Carter peeked up over the mound in front of him. The remains of buildings—all shot up, walls missing, some burned, some people's houses—stood around him. This had once been a prosperous neighborhood in Aleppo, now reduced to shells and remnants. Yet Carter knew people still lived in them, huddling in whatever semisafe place they could find when the fighting came their way.

"What happened?" Carter asked Nemat, who was heading toward him, crouched low as a precaution. Nemat was Jalal's slightly younger brother, and the person in their group who spoke the best English. When Carter had approached the band of men, requesting to be embedded with them so he could report on the Syrian civil war, it had been Nemat who'd agreed to accompany him. He spoke English and had been very helpful. Jalal hadn't been particularly pleased—that had been evident by the heated exchange between the two brothers—but Carter had come to realize it was out of Jalal's concern for his brother's safety. Jalal might have been the older brother, but he was unable to refuse his younger brother anything, and he had taken protective custody of both Nemat and Carter.

"The government forces ran," Nemat said.

Carter saw a man rush out of one of the nearby buildings and level his gun. A bullet whizzed near Carter's ear, and his breath caught in his throat. Without thinking, Carter yanked the gun from Nemat's hands and fired at the man, who dropped like a stone. Carter knew he shouldn't have done that, but within seconds both he and Nemat would have been killed. Carter pulled Nemat into the depression and handed him back his gun. "Good shot," Carter told him.

Nemat looked at Carter quizzically. He fired off what Carter figured was a question in rapid Arabic before returning to English. "You shot him. I didn't."

"I cannot shoot him, remember?" Carter said. "No gun." Nemat's eyes widened and he nodded. Carter hoped he understood what he was saying. It had to be Nemat who killed the other fighter. Carter, being an American, could not get involved directly in the conflict. He was a reporter, and it was his job to report the news and what was happening, not be a part of the action. "We were defending ourselves."

Carter hoped like hell he hadn't inadvertently shot another freedom fighter. If he had, he figured he'd last only long enough for one of the other men to put a bullet in his head.

Nemat peered out over the edge. "He was government," he said and turned around, giving Carter a huge, perfect smile. It was mostly quiet around them. Fighting could be heard in the distance, along with cries and yelling. "You saved my life," Nemat said, and before Carter could think about it, Nemat hugged him around the waist and squeezed tight. "Thank you."

Carter sat completely still, his mind whirling around in circles faster than a chopper blade. Ever since he'd met Nemat, he'd had thoughts about the young man. There were times when he couldn't keep his eyes off him, and yet he knew he had to. Thoughts like that could be very dangerous both for him and for Nemat. No one knew he was gay. Carter had told no one, and now he was regretting that decision on so many levels. He should never have taken this assignment, although it had never been an issue in the past. He'd simply kept his feelings buried and done his job. But Nemat seemed to get under all his defenses. Carter wanted desperately to hug him back, to close his eyes and hold him while the rest of the world fell away. "I did what you'd do for me," Carter whispered.

Yelling permeated the air, high-pitched and excited. He'd been with the group long enough to recognize the sound of joy. The men had been victorious, and they were celebrating. Nemat backed away and climbed out of the depression. Carter sat alone for a few seconds to clear his head. The heat and sun were oppressive, the air dry and hot, but for those few seconds when he'd been with Nemat all of that had disappeared, as had the feel of sand in everything.

"Carter," Jalal said as he peered down at him. He extended his hand, and Carter took it, letting him help him out of the hole and up to what had once been street level, now a barely recognizable mass of blast holes. The other men were crowded around the government soldier, patting Nemat on the back and smiling. Carter stood apart and let the men celebrate while he pulled a small pad from his pocket and began making notes. He'd been struggling for a way to tell the story of what these men were doing. He had plenty of material on their day-to-day lives: fighting, shooting, the smell of death. And here in the desert heat, death had a very definite scent, but how could he describe that to readers? He'd decided to tell the story through one person, and at first he'd picked Jalal, but that wouldn't work. He needed someone he could speak with and who could understand. As his gaze shifted, Carter smiled as he realized the answer had been in front of him all along. As much as he wanted to deny it, the person he needed to tell this story was Nemat.

As if he knew Carter was thinking about him, Nemat walked over to where Carter stood, frantically scribbling as many notes as he could while the incident was still fresh in his mind. Carter saw him out of the corner of his eye, and the thoughts that had been flowing so freely stopped in their tracks.

"Jalal said the government forces have been driven back out of the neighborhood, and other groups are pushing them farther. We need to move and follow them. They are hopeful to defeat the government in this portion of the city and secure it so our people can return." Nemat looked pleased, and Carter knew he should be, but he found it hard to share in Nemat's joy as he looked around at what was left of the area. They were fighting over rubble now. What had once been a prosperous neighborhood would never be the same.

"That's excellent," Carter said. He'd never made any bones about his side in this conflict and where his sympathies lay. He knew he should be dispassionate and report what happened, but this was so much more than just reporting now. Cold, hard facts were a tiny portion of the story. Carter pulled his phone out of his pocket, thankful he'd been in a location the night before where he could charge it. He snapped pictures of the surrounding area as well as pictures of men celebrating in the distance. He didn't want to get too close, but he needed these images to help bring home how personal this conflict was to these men that Americans only heard about on the evening news. Carter took a few more pictures and was about to turn off his phone when he took a chance and snapped a picture of Nemat as he strode back toward the other men. Carter then turned off the phone to save power and placed it in his pocket. He followed Nemat, making sure he had all his things and was ready to go when the men were.

Part of the agreement he had with this team was that he wouldn't slow them down, and even though the heat was oppressive and he was sweating like crazy and had sand stuck to his skin, he made sure he was ready to go. The team passed around jugs of water, and when it was Carter's turn, he drank plenty before passing the container on. These men were like a family—they fought, lived, ate, and joked together. He'd discovered many of them had grown up together, so they knew and trusted each other without hesitation.

Jalal yelled something, and the men all grabbed their hodgepodge of weapons. Jalal walked over to the body of the man Carter had shot and took his rifle and ammunition. He also checked him over for anything else of value. When he was done, Jalal walked to Nemat and handed everything to him, including a nearly new automatic weapon with full ammunition clips. Jalal appeared proud and smiled at his brother. Carter simply observed and made a note in his pad.

Jalal gave another cry, and they fanned out, quickly scouring the nearby buildings. Carter and Nemat were shown to a safe location, and once the men finished securing the area, they headed out.

As they moved, the sounds of fighting got louder and the team became more cautious. They encountered other freedom fighters. Jalal and the other men would converse with them for news and then move on. Eventually they took up a position on the crest of a rise that overlooked what had once been a commercial area of the city. It appeared to Carter that the fighting was now building to building. He made notes while the men took up positions. The fighting was still a ways away, but they needed to be ready. Carter had already seen how this conflict could change on a dime and knew it would happen again.

They remained in position until the sun began to set. The fighting down below had become sporadic, with only occasional gunfire. As the light diminished, the gunfire seemed to die as well. What amazed Carter was that though this was a city, when night fell it was as nearly as dark as uninhabited countryside. Lights shone in a few areas, but only in places where one group or the other held sway and had done so for a longer period of time. He knew some parts of the city hadn't had power at all in months.

Carter could barely see his hand in front of his face. Jalal issued a quiet order, and the men withdrew inside a nearby building. The walls and what was left of the roof gave shelter from the night. Only then did the men break out a small light and pass around what food they had. Carter had learned many of these small freedom-fighting units could only stay in the field for a few days. Then the fighters went home, where they could rest and their families could help replenish their supplies, and then they would return to fight some more. There were no formal supply lines, and no generals calling the shots or trying to build strategy. The groups worked together as best they could, some under regional warlords, but most were bands of independent men fighting for what they believed in.

Carter made his own contribution to the cause of some dried vegetables from his pack, and the men gathered together and ate. They talked quietly, but the camaraderie and shared hardship had bonded these men more closely together even in the relatively short period of time Carter had been with them.

"You tell people about us," Jalal said to him. "Tell them we fight hard."

"I will tell them you fight hard and with heart," Carter said and waited for Nemat to translate for them. They murmured, and Carter saw them all nod. They seemed pleased. Carter had started as a history major but then switched to journalism, and when he'd first taken this assignment, he hadn't been sure what to expect. But now he imagined these men as the modern Middle-East version of the American minutemen. They were fighting for their homes and their freedom. Both Nemat and Jalal were so young—too young. Nemat, he suspected, was about twenty-two, and Jalal only a few years older.

"I speak to you," Jalal whispered to him once everyone had eaten. Carter stood up and followed the large man away from the others. Jalal turned to him and said, "I know what you did with Nemat."

Carter instantly thought someone had seen Nemat embrace him. He opened his mouth to protest that there was nothing wrong; it had only been a hug because Nemat had been grateful. "There was—"

"I know you kill army soldier to protect Nemat," Jalal said.

Carter swallowed. "Did he tell you?"

Jalal shook his head. "I see how Nemat look when I give him…." Jalal motioned handing Nemat the rifle and dead man's possessions. "He look at you."

"I was protecting both of us," Carter explained.

Jalal nodded. "My family, me—we in debt to you. We pay. You are family now." Carter saw Jalal smile in the moonlight. Then Jalal walked back to the group, and Carter followed, wondering what had just happened.

The men were talking quietly, some laughing and joking. Carter had initially thought that strange, but soon realized it was their way of relieving stress. They needed some semblance of normalcy, and acting normal—talking, laughing, playing little jokes on each other, or on the American in their midst—was a way of doing that.

At one point, all of the men looked at each other and stood up. As a group, they all faced the same direction, toward Mecca, knelt, and quietly began to pray. Carter stood away from them to give them privacy. He knew they had missed the multiple calls to prayers that had occurred throughout the rest of the Muslim world that day, and now they were saying their own words of thanks. Carter closed his own eyes and said a few words to the god he'd grown up with.

In the past few years, he hadn't been a religious man, but this experience had touched something inside him. He needed someone to be in charge of things, and he prayed these men would be granted whatever it was they were praying for. When he was done, Carter opened his eyes. Nemat was at the back of the group, kneeling with his head very close to the ground. Carter stared at him for a few seconds. He'd seen the men pray before, but usually he tried to get farther away so as not to intrude. But he had no place to go here.

Carter listened and watched Nemat, his mind filling with thoughts he should not be having, not here, and certainly not while Nemat was praying. Carter turned away and silently found a place to sit. He didn't move or make a sound until the others stood up. Then he opened his pack and pulled out a bedroll. He spread it on the floor and the others did the same. Nemat spread his next to Carter's. Carter lay down and felt Nemat do the same. He wanted to turn toward the wall so he wouldn't be as aware of Nemat next to him, but no one slept with their face away from the door or opening for any reason. It could cost any of them their lives.

In the darkness, Nemat lay just in front of him, his body a dark, alluring curve. Carter closed his eyes and tried to keep his mind on what he was supposed to be doing, the story he was to be working on, the fact that danger lurked just outside the building. Every few minutes, Carter would catch a glimpse of the man standing guard over all of them just outside the door. But no matter how much he tried, his thoughts returned to Nemat and how close he was.

CARTER DIDN'T realize how exhausted he'd been until he woke, cold, sometime in the night. During the day, the temperatures could reach nearly unbearable levels, but at night, in the dry air, they could plummet. He shifted and climbed beneath his single blanket, and that provided some relief for a little while, but then the cold seeped in again.

Nemat moved closer, pulling his bedroll next to Carter. Then he pressed to him, and Carter did his best not to gasp. The other men were moving nearer as well, sharing their bodily warmth against the night's cold. There was nothing remotely sexual about it. They were in a war zone, huddled in a half-destroyed building, trying to keep the cold night air at bay. Carter moved closer to Nemat, inhaling deeply while trying not to make a sound at all.

His head spun when Nemat's manly scent reached his nose. He willed his body not to react, because there would be no hiding it in the position they were lying in. Carter concentrated on the cold and the fact that if anything at all happened, he would certainly be left out in it, in many different ways. Nemat moved closer, and the warmth between them finally began to push away the cold. Carter closed his eyes and willed himself back to sleep. He had to rest, because God knew what the next day would bring.

At some point during the night, Carter heard people shifting in the room and then some shuffling near him. He didn't lift his head. He was too tired, and since there was no cry of alarm, he assumed it was the men changing guard. He went back to sleep. One of the things he'd learned in previous assignments was to pack light. The other was to sleep anywhere. If his back ached, he learned to ignore it and rest. In these kinds of situations, rest periods could come few and far between, so if there was no alarm and no reason to wake, you slept. So that was what he did.

"Carter."

His name whispered softly permeated his sleep-deprived brain. He opened his eyes. Nemat was stirring next to him, and when he sat up, he saw Jalal lying on Nemat's other side. Carter yawned and sat up. The other men were doing the same. His stomach rumbled, and he rummaged in his pack for one of the meal bars he'd brought along. They tasted like dry nothing, but filled his stomach. He drank some water as he stretched out his sore, cramped muscles.

"We need to go soon," Nemat told him.

More than anything at this point, Carter wished for a shower and a proper bathroom. He stepped outside and relieved himself in a place that looked as though others had already done the same. When he returned, Jalal was awakening, stretching and yawning. One of the men brought Jalal something to eat, and he stood up.

Within minutes they'd packed everything away. Light was breaking in the east as the band settled in their positions, weapons at the ready. As the sun rose, Carter kept expecting the fighting to escalate, but the air remained still, with just the slightest dry breeze. He was cold, but he knew he wouldn't remain that way for long.

"What is your family like?" Nemat asked, sitting next to him as they both looked down from their bit of high ground. Classic military strategy dictated that the high positions were the best, but here, the higher positions were also more likely to be bombed from above by Syrian military planes. Carter knew they were taking a chance and that every man in the band was listening carefully for anything that might be flying overhead.

"There's just my mother, dad, and sister," Carter answered. "My sister's older and she's married. She's staying home with the kids, and her husband is a finish carpenter."

"Do they know you are here"—he motioned around—"with us?"

"They know I'm out of the country, but they don't know I'm in Syria." His parents would come unglued if they knew, and the only way he could do this job was with absolute secrecy. "Very few people back home know where I am."

Nemat nodded. "You know what happens if you are caught?"

Carter nodded. "I know." He'd either be taken prisoner, thrown into a Syrian prison, and used for propaganda purposes, or the government would try to get a prisoner from the US for him before releasing him. Since no one in the States would negotiate for his release, if he were caught he'd likely be held for years until either one side or the other prevailed in this conflict, and even then he might never taste freedom again. There was also the more direct approach. "They could shoot me as a spy."

"Why are you doing this, then?" Nemat asked as a shot rang out nearby. Carter jumped slightly, but Nemat didn't even flinch. "This is not your fight."

Carter thought for a few seconds, trying to answer Nemat's question without resorting to meaningless platitudes. "I'm here because back home, what is happening here is very far away. They don't realize what it's like here. They sit in their comfortable homes and talk about freedom and how proud they are to be Americans." Carter lowered his voice when he realized he was beginning to get on his soapbox. "We fought for our freedom many times, and that's what you're doing now. They need to understand why you fight and that you aren't different from us. You're fighting for what we already have."

"But why are *you* here?" Nemat asked.

"I guess I'm here because I need to tell your story. If my people understand, then maybe they'll help you win." He'd come to Syria for many reasons. It was his job, and he lived for the excitement of the assignment. But those reasons had changed over time. Originally, he'd come here because it was his job; he stayed because he believed in the cause… their cause.

"Is there no other reason?" Nemat asked, drilling his gaze into Carter's.

Carter swallowed hard and tried to understand just what Nemat was asking.

Gunfire erupted nearby, and Carter sank to the ground while the men returned fire. He held his hands over his ears as shots continued back and forth. One of the men, Hassan, was hit. He fell back, and within seconds, Carter heard a man scream from behind the mound he was trying to crawl beneath for cover. The firing stopped, and Carter hurried to where Hassan lay on the ground. He had blood on his arm, and Carter pulled him closer for cover and began removing his shirt. Hassan groaned and most likely swore as Carter tried to get to the wound.

"It's a flesh wound. The bullet didn't go in," Carter told Nemat, who translated. Carter grabbed his pack and pulled out his first-aid kit, then cleaned and bandaged the wound. Shots resumed, and the short break in the action was over. Carter helped Hassan back into his shirt. One of the men handed Hassan his rifle, and Hassan went back to his position as though nothing had happened.

The fighting continued off and on for much of the day. Government forces kept trying to take their position, but they were held off. "The men down below as well as us up here keep driving the army back," Nemat told him. The men were getting tired, and Carter wondered how long they could hold this position.

A low-pitched rumble reached Carter's ears. He pulled sunglasses from his pack and put them on, then looked up at the sky. He pointed toward a dark object heading toward them. The others followed his gaze, instantly grabbed their weapons, and raced down the back side of the rise. Carter stayed with Nemat. They were two hundred yards or so away when the first bombs hit, shaking the ground and knocking Carter off his feet. He scrambled back up and continued running after Nemat. They ducked inside a ruined building and pressed to the side of one of the standing walls as another bomb fell. Dust and dirt rained down on them, but by some miracle, the structure held.

"Are you hurt?" Nemat asked.

Carter shook his head as another blast rocked the building. This one was closer and shook the ground and walls. "We need to get out of here. This is going to fall on us," he said. Nemat nodded his agreement and moved toward the opening. Carter followed, and they made their way in the shadows between the buildings, getting farther and farther away. "Do you know where we are?"

Nemat nodded and led on. All Carter could do was follow and hope for the best. It took him a while to realize Nemat was leading him back toward the position they'd defended the day before. They reached the place, but no one else was there. The man he'd shot was gone, blood-soaked ground marking the spot where he'd died. They got into position in the same depression they'd used for cover before and settled in to wait. "Jalal say to come here," Nemat said.

Carter nodded and peered out over and down the pockmarked road, looking for any movement. He saw nothing. He pulled out a bottle of water and drank some before handing the rest to Nemat. He also pulled out a meal bar and handed half to Nemat. He didn't have many left. Once his meager supply was gone, he'd have to figure out a way out of the city and across the Turkish border without getting caught, shot, or dying of thirst.

Neither of them talked while they ate. They were both way too on edge. Thankfully, no opposing forces rumbled down the road toward them, but no one friendly did either. "We should find a better place. This is too open," Carter said, and Nemat looked around, then pointed toward a building. Carter nodded, and they ran toward it and got inside. The door was half off its hinges, but they closed it and took shelter in one of the rooms that overlooked the street. They had a decent vantage point, and as long as no one tried to level the building, they should be safe.

"Stay here," Nemat said, handing Carter his old rifle. Carter nodded and took it. He'd only use it for defense, but he felt better knowing he had it. He looked out the opening, which had once been a window, and when he turned back, Nemat was gone. Carter stared out, ready in case someone came along, but he saw nothing.

It was eerily silent. Not even a bird chirped. The only thing he heard was the occasional rush of air as the desert wind blew down the street. "Nemat," Carter called softly, but he got no response. He wondered where Nemat had gone, and for a few seconds thought he might have been left behind.

After a few minutes, he heard footsteps and whirled around, sighing when he saw Nemat, pleased he hadn't shot him. Nemat was carrying cans, and he handed them to Carter. From the pictures on the labels, Carter was able to deduce what was inside—fruit of some kind. Nemat pulled out a knife and plunged it into the top of one of the cans, then pried open the lid. "Where were they?"

Nemat pointed downward, indicating a basement or cellar of some kind. "There are more," he said with a smile. "I covered the opening so no one can find it but us." He held the open can out to him, and Carter dipped his finger in the sauce. It was sweet and slid smoothly down his throat. He didn't give a damn what was in the can, actually. They could be sweetened scorpions for all he cared. He was so sick of meal bars, he'd eat just about anything.

The contents turned out to be something close to peaches. He and Nemat finished off both cans and then sat on the floor grinning at each other. They took turns watching the road. A few times people ventured out, but never stayed for long. They seemed to be foraging, and Carter hoped they didn't try to get in here. They waited most of the day. In the evening, Nemat left and returned with more cans, which he opened and shared with Carter. Later, he returned with a jar of olives, and Carter thought he'd died and gone to heaven.

"What are your father and mother like?" Nemat asked once they were both full.

"He's a mechanic. Fixes cars," Carter explained. "Mom is a nurse in a hospital. They wanted both of us to get an education, so we could make something more of ourselves."

"They educated your sister?" Nemat asked. "There are those here who feel teaching women is wrong. But I think they are wrong." Carter nodded. "My father was a diplomat, so we spent time in Canada. I went to school there," Nemat said proudly. "Jalal went too, but he didn't want to learn English or anything about life in Canada."

"What about your mother?"

Nemat shook his head, and Carter got the message. "She was a very good mother. She loved Jalal and me very much. My father died too. So now I have Jalal. He is my family."

"Are there uncles and cousins?" Carter asked, concerned that Nemat and Jalal had no one except each other. The thought of anything happening to either of them sent a shock through Carter's heart.

"Yes, many," Nemat said. "But a lot have died in this fighting. Even more will die before the fighting ends." He didn't have to say he hoped neither he nor Jalal were among them; that was clear from Nemat's expression.

"Should we try to find them?" Carter asked, peering out at the deserted street.

"They will come here," Nemat said confidently.

The sun set quickly, and soon they were thrust into near total darkness. They moved farther into what had once been a house and found a room that seemed safe. Carter got his bedroll out of his pack and spread it on the floor. He then sat on it. Nemat did the same, except he oriented his toward Mecca and began to pray. Carter closed his eyes and listened as Nemat quietly said his prayers. Then, once he was done, Carter heard him moving in the darkness. The cold of night would quickly permeate the house, so Carter helped Nemat place his bedroll next to his, and then they both lay down.

Carter closed his eyes, figuring he might as well sleep. As dark as it was, they weren't going to see anyone, but they'd certainly hear anyone who tried to approach them. They seemed safe enough for now.

The cold quickly made its way to them, and soon Nemat pressed against him. Carter moved closer as well and felt Nemat roll over. He held still and waited, wondering what was going on.

"I see you sometimes," Nemat said in a whisper.

Carter wondered what he meant until Nemat moved closer and he felt Nemat's breath on his skin. Carter stiffened and shivered, but not from the cold. He went completely still. Then Nemat kissed him. Nemat immediately pulled back and seemed to be waiting for Carter to say or do something. Carter couldn't even hear him breathe. He reached out and located Nemat's head and then cheeks, caressing him gently before guiding their lips back together.

Nemat moved closer, deepening the kiss only slightly. Both of them were tentative, and Carter had no idea if he should take things further or not until the tiniest of moans reached his ears and was instantly cut off.

Carter pulled Nemat closer and held him tighter, feeling his excitement through his clothes. Nemat deepened the kiss, pressing still nearer as Carter hugged him closer. He knew this could be a massive mistake, regardless of whether Nemat had instigated it or not. If they were caught, Carter would be killed, and Nemat's family would claim Carter had ruined him. Nemat would face trouble, but Carter had no doubt who would be blamed. Still, he'd spent weeks watching Nemat, dreaming of how he would taste, and now he had his answer: incredible. Carter deepened the kiss and lightly stroked Nemat through his clothing.

Nemat shivered, pressing forward for more. Carter carefully and slowly opened Nemat's pants, pulled him out, and slowly stroked him. Nemat shook like a leaf in the wind. He broke the kiss and gasped for air. When Nemat's lips returned, they tasted slightly of blood, and Carter knew Nemat had bitten his lip to keep from crying out.

Carter moved away slightly, opened his pants, and pulled himself out. He wrapped his hands around both of their lengths. Nemat kissed him hard and began to thrust. Carter did the same. They would both probably have been moaning and whimpering like crazy, but their kisses swallowed the sounds and the room remained silent except for their breathing. It wasn't long before Nemat whimpered, and Carter tightened his hands around both of them, their cocks sliding past each other.

The sensation was sublime, and Carter wished he could see Nemat's face, his eyes. He wanted to know what Nemat looked like right now. Nemat gasped and then Carter felt him come. Carter followed right behind him, trying his best not to scream his passion into the night.

Nemat stilled, and after a few minutes, Carter could almost feel the shame creep into Nemat's body, because it worked its way into his as well.

"Jalal," Nemat said quietly.

"It's okay," Carter said, searching for something in his pack that he could use to clean them up. The last thing he needed was for someone to find them looking or smelling debauched. He found a small wad of paper and used it to wipe himself before handing it to Nemat. Then he felt Nemat shift away and heard him doing up his clothes. Carter did the same and lay back down.

Nemat said nothing, but the cold drove them together. Carter lay with Nemat pressed next to him. He reached out and lightly stroked Nemat's arm to try to comfort him. He heard him sigh softly, but Nemat didn't pull away. For that small favor Carter was grateful. He knew guilt could be a tough thing to get beyond, but at least Nemat didn't hate him. Carter yawned and closed his eyes. In the dark he'd had everything he'd imagined. But the morning and the light would change everything. He had no doubts about that, and it couldn't be helped, no matter how much he wished he could change things. He and Nemat could hide, maybe even pretend in the dark, but in the bright light of day, nothing of what they'd done could make an appearance. Carter sighed and tried his best to settle his mind and get some sleep.

CHAPTER TWO

CARTER WOKE when Nemat shifted next to him. He peered out the doorway and through the house to where light was just starting to filter into the room. He sat up, stretched, and stood. Within minutes, both he and Nemat had silently packed up. He stowed everything in his pack and picked up the rifle Nemat had given him. They crept through the house and glanced out the window. The street was still deserted, but a few signs of life appeared in the silent morning.

"We cannot stay here much longer," Carter said, and Nemat nodded. He left and returned with two more cans of food. After opening them, the two of them ate in silence. Carter could see the shame in Nemat's eyes and wished he could soothe it away, but he had no idea what to say. They both remained silent for a long time.

"There's nothing to be ashamed of," Carter finally said.

"We cannot speak of it," Nemat told him, pointing outside. "There are many ears." He smiled slightly, and some of Carter's trepidation melted away. They watched the road until Nemat burst into a grin. Jalal, Hassan, and the other men turned the corner down the road. Nemat made a soft sound, and the group walked toward the house. Carter and Nemat got the door open, and the band of men walked inside to warm greetings. Nemat and Jalal talked hurriedly, and then Nemat left the room. He returned with still more cans of food, which he passed out. It seemed they were coming to the end of the good stuff, but everyone ate his fill and then they left the house, following Jalal.

Carter wasn't sure where they were headed, but he kept his eyes peeled for trouble. He'd returned the rifle to Nemat, grateful he hadn't had to use it again.

Jalal caught Nemat's eye and walked over to speak to his brother.

"We're going to meet with one of the warlords," Nemat whispered to him after Jalal moved farther away from them. Carter wasn't particularly thrilled at that news. "We will wait while Jalal speaks to the commander. Then we are going back to our family." Nemat seemed quite pleased at the news. "You will come with us?"

Carter needed to figure out a way to get out of the country and back into Turkey. He could not afford to have the tide of the conflict turn and find himself at the mercy of the government. He'd hoped he could mix in with a group of refugees and get out of the country that way. But he found himself agreeing and was pleased when he found that Nemat's family lived in the general direction he needed to go. "Jalal says you are family now," Nemat told him with a smile.

"I would be pleased to meet your family," Carter told him.

They walked for quite a distance until they were all picked up by a truck headed out of the city. Jalal explained to the driver where they needed to go, and he motioned them into the back of the truck. They headed down streets strewn with rubble, past buildings reduced to piles next to ones that appeared largely unscathed. Eventually the truck slowed down, and Jalal got out. He spoke to the driver and handed something to him, probably some form of payment. The driver nodded and settled in to wait.

Carter took the opportunity to make notes on his pad, which was rapidly filling. He had four more just like it in the bottom of his pack, already filled, along with photos he'd stored on a hidden flash card to document what he'd seen. He had one last blank notebook in the pack, and it looked like he would need it very soon.

They waited an hour or so, and then Jalal returned. He seemed pleased and jumped in the back of the truck, then banged lightly on the cab. The truck began to move, and they continued their journey out of the war-ravaged city and into the desert countryside.

"Does Jalal know the driver?" Carter asked Nemat.

Nemat translated, and the men all laughed. They talked back and forth for a few minutes while Carter waited. He had picked up a number of language skills over the past few weeks, and he could pick out the occasional phrase or word, but they were speaking too fast for him to catch on to most of what was being said.

"He is taking us just a few more miles," Nemat told him. "They thought it funny that you asked if we knew the driver."

"I don't understand," Carter said.

"He is a freedom fighter like us. So he is like a brother," Nemat said, and Carter nodded. After a while, the truck pulled off the road, and they climbed out. The driver waved and turned around, heading back toward the city while they walked toward the horizon. "It isn't far," Nemat assured him.

Carter hoped that was true. The heat was oppressive, with no relief or shade. He drained the last of his water, and the others were doing the same. A cloud of dust rose in the distance, and they all leapt off the road for cover. A small truck appeared out of the cloud, and the men called out and jumped from their positions. Carter wondered what was happening, but then realized the man in the truck was a relative who had been sent to come find them. They all jumped in the back and set their gear on the floor of the truck bed. The truck turned around, and they sped off toward what initially appeared as a blip on the horizon, but soon materialized into a small town.

The men began to chant and cry out with joy, obviously happy to be home.

The truck pulled into the center of a cluster of buildings. Doors opened, and people flooded out into the street, all talking excitedly. As the men jumped down, each was greeted and welcomed back. Hassan got special attention and was fussed over because of his wound. When Carter climbed down, most looked at him in wonder. Jalal and Nemat motioned him over to where a middle-aged man stood. They both spoke to him, and Jalal pointed toward him. Carter nodded slightly. He was obviously being introduced. "This is our uncle, Nasim," Nemat told him.

"Jalal says you are a member of our family now," Nasim said in clear English, with a measured tone. Carter wasn't sure if that was because of the unfamiliar language or reservations on his part. Not that Carter could blame him. This was a country in crisis, fighting a civil war. They had reason to be suspicious of strangers.

"I am honored," Carter told him, inclining his head as a show of respect.

Nasim pointed toward a nearby house. Carter assumed he was to go that way. Thankfully, Nemat and Jalal went along as well.

Shade-cooled air greeted him when he stepped inside. It felt amazing, and some of the tension he'd been holding drifted away. He noticed that the house had electricity.

"This area has been under our control for almost a year now," Nemat told Carter when he mentioned it. "So we have reliable electricity, and the provincial government is friendly to our cause." Nemat led him through the house to a small room. "This is where you will stay when you are here. There is a bathing room right here," he told Carter and opened a door. The bathroom had a claw-footed tub that must have been fifty years old. Not that it mattered—Nemat turned on the water and it ran. Carter nearly collapsed in joy. "The family will be gathering at sundown," Nemat said. "Until then you will be able to bathe and rest. Fresh clothes will be put in your room."

"Thank you," Carter said, and Nemat smiled in return. He could still see the nervousness and shame in his eyes and wished he could pull Nemat close and somehow make that disappear, but he couldn't. There was nothing he could do except kick himself over and over for causing those feelings.

"I will leave you now, but come to the room where we entered when you are ready," Nemat said. Carter nodded and set his pack near the bed in the small bedroom he'd been given. The room was nice, clean, and smelled fresh. At that point, he realized how much *he* stank. Carter wanted to get out of these clothes and clean up so badly he could taste it.

A knock sounded on the door, and an old woman entered. She smiled at him, showing her few remaining teeth. She set a small stack of clothes on the bed. Carter thanked her, hoping she understood the tone if not the words. Carter picked up the clothes as well as his pack and went into the bathroom. He closed the door and ran some water. He didn't use a lot because of the preciousness of that resource. Then he stripped off his clothes and climbed into the tub.

A cloth had been provided for him, along with a tiny bar of soap. Carter used both, and within minutes he was clean and the water in the bottom of the tub was gray. He stood up and let the water sluice off him. Then he drained the water and stood in the center of the room, the dry air from the high window evaporating the moisture faster than any towel.

Carter dug in his pack for the few toiletries he'd brought. He combed his hair and thoroughly brushed his teeth before shaving as best he could. He wished he'd remembered to do that while he was in the bath, but at least once he was done, he looked presentable. The robes that had been brought for him were old, but very soft, and felt luxurious on his skin after spending almost a week in the same clothes. He walked back to the bedroom he'd been given to use. He wondered what he should do with his dirty clothes. His first instinct was to have them burned, and maybe he would once he got back to Turkey. For now, he placed them on top of his pack, then did as Nemat had told him and retraced his steps to the front room.

Nemat and Jalal were seated on cushions on the floor. They both looked clean as well. Carter wondered how big the house was and how many bathrooms it had. But he kept himself from asking the question, in case it was rude. Carter sat where Jalal indicated, and they were soon joined by Nasim, who retrieved a hookah from the corner of the room and moved it into the center. He lit it with a deft hand and handed one of the tubes to Carter.

Carter had never been a smoker of any kind, but this was an honor and it would be rude of him to reject the hospitality, so he took the tube and inhaled gently. The few times he'd tried tobacco he'd hated it, but this was mild and seemed more like a flavor and less like smoke. To his surprise, he enjoyed it, so he slowly inhaled again. Then he passed the stem to Nemat.

After being passed the pipe tube a few times, Carter felt incredibly mellow. He didn't know what they'd been smoking, and he didn't care. Food was brought: hummus, olives, rice with meat, pita bread. His stomach rumbled, and he was encouraged to eat.

"These are hard times for my country," Nasim said.

"Many in my country understand and sympathize with your plight," Carter said. "That's why I'm here, so I can return and try to explain what is happening and what we can do to help."

Nasim nodded. "We will drive the oppressor out, and then we will create a country of our own that exists for all of us and not just the Alawites." Nemat's uncle nearly spat when he said the last word. Then he schooled his expression. "Have you gotten what you needed?" Nemat began speaking rapidly, and Carter wondered what was being said. One thing was for sure—before he took another assignment like this, he was most definitely going to learn the language. He'd been lucky locating Jalal and Nemat. He probably wouldn't be so lucky the next time. "Nemat says there are things you must be shown before you leave."

"Graves," Nemat said. "People killed by the government, all buried together."

"Eat," Nasim told them all, and the conversation ground to a halt.

They spent hours in quiet, smoking a little and eating a whole lot. Carter was simply happy for the quiet. But no matter how content he was, he couldn't help being aware of Nemat seated right next to him.

Nasim eventually stood up. "Rest. You have been gone a long time."

Carter wondered if he was being told to go to his room, but Nemat and Jalal simply relaxed back on the large cushions. Soon, their eyes had drifted shut. Carter felt unbelievably comfortable, and soon his eyes drifted closed as well.

He didn't sleep for long, but he felt better when he woke. The others had stirred as well. One thing was certain. In the heat of this part of the world, western clothes were a real pain in the ass. The robes he wore were comfortable, flowing, and allowed his skin to breathe. He didn't feel sweaty and uncomfortable in the least, even though it was hot. More food and drink were delivered to them, and the old woman who had brought him the clothes came into the room and said something to Nemat. He smiled and stood up, then hugged her tightly.

"This is my grandmother," Nemat explained. Carter stood and nodded reverently to her. "She says she has washed your clothes and placed them back in your room."

"Thank you," Carter said with a smile, and she returned it before leaving again. They ate some more, and when offered this time, Carter passed on the pipe. He needed his wits about him, and something in that smoke was most definitely off.

The light outside had begun to fade before both Nemat and Jalal got up. "We are expected in the courtyard for a celebration," Nemat told Carter. "They are happy that we have returned."

"Do they celebrate every time you come home?"

"Yes. They do not know when will be the last time," Nemat said. Carter looked over at Jalal, who nodded. *What a way to live.* He understood the logic—being thankful for what you had and celebrating it because it might all be taken away. But it seemed like a difficult way to live.

What Carter presumed was most of Nemat and Jalal's extended family waited for them in the courtyard. Tables had been set up with still more food. In a country torn by war, he had to wonder where it had come from, but he wasn't about to ask. It was none of his business, and it would be seen as an intrusion. The thing he did notice was that there was very little meat of any kind, and most of the dishes were made with ingredients that could be easily stored or preserved.

The family members cheered, and the boys and men clapped the fighters on the shoulder. They were being treated like heroes, and that warmed Carter's heart. They *were* heroes, fighting for what they believed in so their families and children might have a chance at a better life.

The celebration really took off. People talked and laughed, eating and drinking. He knew no alcohol was being served, but the fruit-and-yogurt-based drinks went down smooth and easy. Carter spent much of the evening watching everyone. He rarely took part in things. The reporter in him was very much an observer. When musicians began to play, people danced. The women largely kept to the side while the men made merry. Carter had noticed that while the women didn't wear the traditional burka, they did dress sedately and were nearly completely covered. He saw no harem girls or belly dancers here.

Once everyone seemed to have eaten their fill, the women began carrying things away. Carter watched and realized the family might have put out a huge spread as a show of celebration, but not a scrap of that food would go to waste. People quietly began filtering home.

Carter watched Nemat and took his cue from him as to when it was time to leave. He'd been introduced to everyone even though he couldn't remember their names, but they knew his. He said good night to each person as they said good night to him, and then he walked back to the house. He said good night to Jalal and Nemat before he went to the room he'd been given to use and closed the door. He found his clothes had been set on his pack, folded and clean. Another robe had also been placed on the small chair, and he figured that was for the morning. He stripped off his clothes and pulled on the clean underwear, then pulled back the sheets to check for unwanted visitors and got in bed. He was asleep within seconds.

He didn't know how long he'd been asleep, but he woke to someone else in the room. "Who is it?" Carter whispered.

"It is me," Nemat told him before coming forward. "I hope it is safe to speak now." Carter sat up and heard Nemat move closer. "You are not the first person I met who is like me, but you are the first I do anything with," Nemat said.

"Does anyone in your family know?" Carter asked, already fairly sure of the answer.

"No. I met a boy named Mark when I was in Canada. He explained things to me, so I understand. But then we came back home, and you are the first man like me I have met." Nemat chuckled softly. "Actually, I know of other men like me, but they have wives."

"So you aren't racked with guilt over what happened?"

"No. I was shocked and scared because we cannot be discovered, but I do not feel guilty." Nemat leaned closer. "That is why I do this," Nemat said before kissing him. Carter reached out to pull Nemat into an embrace, but Nemat stopped him. "I must go. We stay here tomorrow, but the day after that, I will show you the graves you need to see. There are places that are private, where no one goes." Nemat stood up, and Carter watched as Nemat silently opened the door and stepped out, then closed the door behind him.

Carter stared at the closed door, wondering what the hell had just happened. In his mind, Nemat had always been this innocent kid who needed protection, but obviously Nemat knew more about the world than he let on. Maybe that was how he protected himself from an environment that would be incredibly hostile to who he was. Carter settled onto the bed and tried his best not to think about the fact that his dick could pound nails. He could still taste Nemat on his lips. He ran his tongue over them to enjoy the flavor before he closed his eyes and drifted back to sleep. Hopefully he'd be able to dream of Nemat and whatever it was he had in mind for them on this trip he'd planned to show Carter something he needed to see.

THE NEXT day, no one seemed to go very far from the small compound of houses. Nemat and Jalal stayed busy, most likely with chores their aunts had asked them to complete. They also wandered through the family's olive grove. Carter spent some time with Nasim, but they didn't speak much, and Carter got the feeling Nasim wasn't quite sold on him yet. That was okay. Carter believed trust needed to be built and earned. He'd done that with Nemat and Jalal. They'd been together twenty-four hours a day for the past two weeks, learning to rely on and trust each other. Both brothers knew Carter had saved Nemat's life, even if the rest of the family didn't.

There wasn't a lot for him to do, and every time he turned around he was being fed or offered something to drink. Carter knew that was part of the hospitality of their culture, but he was a very active person, and sitting around for an entire day was hard for him. He spent part of the day organizing his notes. He was also able to charge his phone, and he managed to download the pictures to a flash drive he kept hidden in the bottom of his pack as a precaution. By the end of the day, he was rested, clean, and full, so basically he felt better than he had since he'd crossed the border into Syria.

That night he didn't have a repeat visitor in his room, but Carter thought about Nemat almost constantly. During the day, whenever Nemat wasn't doing chores, they'd spent time together talking about little things that seemed to fascinate the other. But in that time, Nemat had laughed, really laughed, more than once, and he'd smiled almost constantly. That alone made it a good day, and one Carter would always remember.

The following morning, Nemat knocked on his door. Carter was already up and dressed. They got ready and left early before the heat of the day could set in. They were both dressed in old clothes, and Nemat steered him toward a pickup truck that had definitely seen better days. "It looks ugly, but it runs good," Nemat had told him earlier, and he hadn't lied. The engine purred like a kitten, even if the body looked about ready to fall to pieces.

"Where are we going?" Carter asked once they were on the road. At first they'd headed toward the city, but then Nemat had turned off the road and headed north along a track that looked about ready to disappear into the desert at any time. "Is it safe?"

"No one goes here. They say restless spirits stay here." Nemat grinned at him. "I know that's nonsense, but no one comes here. They are afraid." They crested a rise, and then Nemat pulled to a stop.

Carter wasn't sure what he was looking at. It looked like a large depression created by wind-blown sand. Nemat got out and pulled out the shovel from the back of the truck. He handed it to Carter. "Go down there and dig a single shovelful."

Carter understood that Nemat was taking him to a cemetery. He swallowed, but did as Nemat asked. He descended the slight hill and dug into the dry ground. He got only earth. He dug again, making a slight hole. Something moved. He dug down further and uncovered the remnants of what looked to him to be a desiccated arm. Carter pulled out his phone and snapped a picture, making sure it was clear exactly what was in the picture. He had seen a lot of dead bodies, but this sent a chill down his spine. If all he'd had to do was dig a few shovelfuls of dirt to uncover a corpse, what else was buried in this place? How many people had been dumped here? And over how much time?

He looked around, then began taking photographs of the surrounding landmarks. He had to document the location. "What do you call this place?" he asked Nemat, but Nemat just shrugged.

"It doesn't have a name, just like the people," Nemat told him. Carter pulled out his notebook and frantically took notes. Using his phone again, he took GPS coordinates and jotted them down. At least now the location would be known, no matter how much the wind shifted the sand. "We should go," Nemat called. Carter climbed back up to where Nemat waited. "The government will not be happy we are here."

"I thought the freedom fighters were in control of this area," Carter said.

"They are, but that doesn't mean there aren't people loyal to Assad," Nemat explained. There wasn't much more Carter could do here anyway, so he motioned to the truck, and Nemat led the way back. They got in, and Carter looked around for any sign of anyone else. He saw nothing, but Nemat was right—someone could be watching or they could see the truck. It was best not to linger.

Nemat turned the truck around, and they headed back the way they came. When they reached the point where they'd turned off, Nemat turned farther away from the compound. Neither of them spoke. Carter certainly wasn't in the mood as he pondered the ramifications of what he'd found.

"Look there," Nemat said, pointing ahead. Buildings broke the horizon, and as they got closer, a compound came into view. Carter saw a large building with a wall around it. "A member of Assad's family built it, but it was never finished." Nemat turned in and parked behind the wall. "No one comes here."

"Why would anyone build in the middle of nowhere like this?" Carter asked.

"There used to be a spring here, but it's gone now," Nemat said.

Carter looked around at the concrete shell of the building with the remnants of trees, brown and very dead, partially buried in sand. Nemat reached behind the truck seat and pulled out a small bag. He then led the way inside.

There wasn't much to see other than a few walls, vacant doorways, and holes where windows should be. Anything of value had been stripped away long ago. The sounds of their footsteps bounced off the empty walls as they walked. Nemat led him to a large, central room with high ceilings. It was dark and surprisingly cool relative to the blazing outdoor sun. "I wanted a place where we could be alone," Nemat explained.

Carter nodded as Nemat pulled a couple blankets out of the bag and spread them on the floor. "Nemat, you don't have to do this," he said. He knew what this meant for Nemat, and what it could mean for both of them if they were caught.

Nemat stepped closer, staring at Carter, who returned the look. "If you do not want me, I understand," Nemat whispered.

"It's not that," Carter said, struggling to decide what was right.

"I hide myself all the time," Nemat said. "My uncle says I must get married. He is starting the search for my wife. I cannot tell him I don't want a wife, because that will make him suspicious, so I say I must wait until after we have won our freedom. That makes him happy. But there is no one to make me happy. Until you." Carter gasped. "I will bring shame to my family if they learn about me. But I know they are wrong. I saw that when I was in Canada. I know there is more than what is allowed here." He moved closer. "I have never told anyone this before." Nemat bit his lower lip, and Carter reached out, lightly tracing the teeth-bruised flesh.

Carter stared into Nemat's deep brown eyes and then looked over his rich light-brown skin. Slowly, he stroked Nemat's cheeks. Some of the men wore beards, but Nemat didn't, and for that Carter was grateful. Nemat appeared innocently and richly beautiful. Carter was so screwed. No matter what happened, he knew he was going to end up very disappointed and most likely hurt… or worse. He moved nearer, as if Nemat were a magnet and he steel. Nemat stepped closer, and Carter pulled him to him, forgetting about everything. When they separated, Nemat tugged him down into the blankets. They kissed again, and Carter savored

Nemat's manly flavor combined with the lingering taste of the spices from what he'd eaten for breakfast.

Nemat moaned softly and stopped. They both listened to the wind and heard nothing more. Carter kissed him again, and Nemat whimpered, then moaned once again, this time into Carter's mouth. They were both taking a chance, but Carter needed this. As soon as Nemat kissed him, Carter needed Nemat's taste, his touch, his scent, as much as he needed air to breathe. They rested on their sides, and Carter tugged Nemat closer, sliding his hand beneath Nemat's shirt to his smooth and soft bare skin beneath.

Carter groaned as he stroked Nemat's hot skin, sliding his hand up Nemat's back and then down over the curve of his bubble butt. Nemat vibrated with an excitement that took Carter right along with him. When they stopped kissing long enough to breathe, Carter sat up, and Nemat did the same. Carter tugged off Nemat's shirt, marveling at his smooth skin. He licked down Nemat's neck and then along his chest, sucking and licking both nipples as Nemat moaned and whimpered softly. Carter pulled off his own shirt and hugged Nemat to him, skin to skin for the first time.

He wasted no time getting as much skin to touch as he could. Carter had no illusions that this could last between them—the gulf was simply too wide—so he memorized each curve and tiny imperfection in Nemat's skin that made him seem even more perfect and remarkably more memorable. He never wanted to forget this moment with Nemat, and in his mind the abandoned building became a palace and Nemat's moans the finest music. They slowly sank back down onto the blankets.

This time Nemat took the initiative, and Carter felt him work open the catch of his pants. Carter sucked in his belly and held still as excitement sang through him. He needed Nemat to touch him. Nemat slipped Carter's pants down his hips, and Carter gasped as Nemat slid his hands over him. He hoped, prayed, and waited for Nemat to touch him, but he seemed to take his time, roaming over Carter's hips and belly, stroking his skin.

"You're so soft," Nemat whispered. "I always thought a man should be hard and rough, but you aren't."

"Neither are you," Carter countered, stroking Nemat's back. Nemat hummed his agreement, and Carter slipped Nemat's pants down his legs.

Nemat shifted, pressing Carter onto his back. He kissed him and situated his hips so their cocks lined up with each other, sliding deliciously along each other so that whenever he moved, Carter got a jolt of pleasure that ran from his hips to his head. Damn, this was perfect. He wished he could stay like this all day.

"Is this good?" Nemat whispered.

"It's perfect," Carter whispered in return and cupped Nemat's butt, pressing them more tightly together. He loved the heat that rolled off Nemat's skin. Hell, he loved the look of him, the feel of him, the taste of him. Carter's head throbbed with unabashed excitement. He wanted more, needed more.

"Is this all?" Nemat asked, and Carter chuckled.

Carter slowly rolled Nemat onto his back, kissed him deeply, and then lightly licked down his skin. There was no way he wanted to raise any kind of mark, so he was extra careful as he licked and sucked his way down Nemat's neck and throat. He laved attention on Nemat's chest, tasting the salt on his skin. Nemat's belly skittered and the muscles rolled as Carter sucked a trail along his abs and into his belly button. Then he continued lower. Nemat's cock throbbed and bounced against his belly. When Carter licked up the length, Nemat let out a high-pitched moan.

Carter smiled and did it again before opening his mouth and sucking in the reddish-brown head of Nemat's cock. Nemat nearly came unglued. The sounds and small cries filled the otherwise empty room. Nemat quieted quickly but shook on the blanket.

"Is this okay?" Carter asked, wrapping his hand around Nemat's length.

Nemat's eyes widened and he nodded. Carter smiled and slowly took him into his mouth again. Nemat's flavor burst on his tongue, salty, sweet, and tangy. Carter took as much as he could and held still, then retreated, letting Nemat's skin drag over his tongue. Carter's cock throbbed as he continued sucking Nemat. Never in his life had he seen or heard anything as sexy and hot as the little sounds Nemat made or the way he moved his hips just a little in order to get more of what he wanted. Carter bobbed his head, sucking and licking to his heart's content. He paused, stroking slowly but firmly before sucking him deep and hard.

Nemat wouldn't last much longer; Carter could tell simply by the way Nemat shook beneath him. Carter paused and let Nemat slip from his lips. He lunged forward, bringing their lips together in a searing kiss that stole his breath with the energy and power that passed between them.

"Carter," Nemat whimpered.

Carter kissed him again before sliding back down his body and sucking Nemat down his throat. He took it all, burying his nose in the black curls at the base of Nemat's cock. Carter inhaled and got a shot of pure musk. He moaned around Nemat's cock, using his tongue as well as his lips to provide as much sensation as possible.

Nemat whimpered, and Carter felt him stiffen and shiver. He knew he was close. "It's okay. Let it all go," Carter told him and sucked him down. Nemat took his advice to heart. His hips rocked and he pressed forward, moaning softly with each thrust. Carter slid his lips all the way down, sucking and licking until Nemat stilled. Carter waited and then swallowed as Nemat came. He took it all, swallowing and sucking until Nemat lay on the blanket, spent and limp. Carter didn't move for a few seconds and then slowly let Nemat's length slip from his lips.

When Carter met Nemat's gaze, he appeared glassy-eyed, his lips parted and curled into a slight smile. "That was…." Nemat smiled more broadly. "I do not have words."

"That's good," Carter told him, kissing him lightly before resting his head on Nemat's belly. Neither of them moved for a while, Nemat sated and exhausted, Carter happy and content. He listened for any sort of sound, but all he heard was the occasional whistle of the breeze as it blew around the remnants of the building.

"Carter," Nemat whispered. "What about you?" Carter hummed softly, and Nemat shifted from under him. Before Carter could react, Nemat had him pressed down onto the blankets. He gasped and the breath flew from his lungs when Nemat first tasted him. Carter wasn't a virgin, but his experience had been limited to mostly quick encounters.

Nemat took him in his mouth. Carter gasped and tried not to scream his pleasure all the way back to the city. He reminded himself about where he was and what would happen if they were caught. That was enough to temper his excitement slightly.

"Take it easy," Carter soothed when Nemat tried to go too fast, and then he closed his eyes as Nemat settled into a steady rhythm. Within seconds, Carter began to float, loving every touch and sensation. He was almost ashamed of how quickly he teetered on the edge and then tumbled over. Carter tried to give Nemat warning, but there was no time. He came hard and fell back once the excitement ebbed.

Gasping for air, he settled back on the blankets and held Nemat close while they kissed, stroking his skin, enjoying the lovely afterglow.

A sound from outside alerted him that something was wrong. Carter stilled and waited. Nemat must have heard it as well, because he sat up and then jumped to his feet. He pulled up his pants and checked his clothes. Carter's heart pounded as he did the same. Nemat rolled the blankets into a ball and shoved them back into his bag before dropping it in the corner of the room. Then he led the way back out toward where the truck was parked.

Men with machine guns stood near the truck; Carter saw them through the glassless window opening. He glanced at Nemat, who looked back at him. "Do you know them?"

Nemat shook his head, then stepped into the doorway and slowly walked toward the men. Nemat spoke to them for a few minutes. Carter moved back into the house and pressed his back to a wall, remaining out of sight. He had no idea whether Nemat wanted him to be seen. He knew being a foreigner could lead to suspicion whether these were freedom fighters, who could very well act on their own, or government soldiers, whom he must not encounter because he was not supposed to be in the country at all. He'd really fucked up this time, and Nemat would pay the price right along with him. He stood still and waited, but heard nothing.

A few minutes later, voices infiltrated the house. They didn't seem loud or menacing. He did recognize Nemat's voice, which sounded normal and relaxed. Carter continued waiting and eventually heard footsteps approach, stop, and then retreat. He stayed where he was, with his back to the wall, unable to move or breathe.

A shot rang out, followed by another, and Carter jumped a little and held his breath, hoping like hell it wasn't Nemat they were shooting at. It sounded like they were right outside the room he was standing in. He didn't hear any more footsteps, or other noise, for that matter. He heard a muffled sound, like someone struggling. He moved away from the wall and peered around the corner. What he saw made his blood run cold. Nemat sat pressed to the outside wall, a man standing over him, pointing a rifle at him.

Nemat looked scared to death, and from his posture, the other man seemed completely in control. Carter wished he had something at hand to subdue the man. More shots rang out from outside, and Carter silently moved back into hiding, praying that whatever was happening would be over soon. An additional shot rang out, and then Carter heard shouting followed by something in a snapped tone from the other room. He heard Nemat say yes, and then footsteps approached. Carter got ready to pounce. His only advantage was surprise. He waited, ready to leap, but then the footsteps got softer and eventually faded away.

Voices sounded outside, men calling back and forth. Carter steadied his breath and waited. Once he no longer heard them, he ventured another look into the next room. "Nemat," Carter said, rushing toward where Nemat still sat against the wall. "Are you okay? Did they hurt you?"

"No," Nemat answered. "They didn't hurt me."

"Did they leave?" Carter asked, chancing a look outside. He saw nothing but Nemat's old truck parked inside the wall. "It looks like they're gone." Nemat nodded. "Who were they? Government?"

"No. They weren't government," Nemat said, sucking in a breath. Then slowly he stood up, but appeared wobbly. Carter steadied him and then gave him some room. Slowly Nemat walked back though the house and retrieved the bag. Then he silently led the way out of the house and to the truck. Carter thanked the powers that be that the truck was still intact. "We need to go now," Nemat said.

"What were all those shots?" Carter asked. "I was afraid they were shooting at you."

"I am fine. You are fine. That is all that counts. We must leave this place now. Forget whatever you saw or heard here. Forget everything." Nemat pulled open the truck door. "Please. We must go."

Carter turned back toward the shell of a building, then shifted his gaze to Nemat before looking at the building again. Then he walked closer and peered around the side. He gasped at the sight and nearly lost what he had in his stomach. Two bodies lay crumpled at the base of the house.

"Please, we must leave now," Nemat said. Carter's reporter instincts and his sense of self-preservation warred with each other. The reporter would have won if Nemat hadn't been with him, but he turned away, dashed back to the truck, and got in the passenger seat. "Get down in case they watch us go," Nemat said, and Carter settled on the floor of the passenger seat as Nemat started the engine, pulled the truck out, and got back on the road.

"Is it safe?" Carter asked. Nemat was driving like the hounds of hell were after him.

"Yes," he said, slowing down. Carter got up and sat on the seat. "What happened back there?" He was met with silence. "Tell me what was going on. Why did that man have a gun on you?" Carter let some of his frustration show through.

"He did not want me to see," Nemat said. "He knew I was not government and he had heard of my uncle, but he did not want me to know what they were doing."

"Nemat, I saw the bodies beside the house. I know they were executed. What I want to know is why." The reporter in him was out in full force.

"I do not know. They did not tell me why. I am just grateful they did not kill me and search the house. I told them I was alone and had taken shelter from the sun to eat before driving the rest of the way home. They asked if I had searched the house, and I said I had. They knew I was a fighter because they knew of Jalal, and I told them I was his brother. They know of our band. After that, they took me in that room and held me while the other men did what they said they had to do."

"Were the men they killed government soldiers? They weren't in uniform."

"They called them—" Nemat paused in his speech and continued driving. "I do not know the word in English. It means outside of God—shameful, really bad." Nemat continued driving. "These men had done something very bad, and they were killed for it and left in the desert. It isn't likely they will be found, so they will not be buried in time and their spirits will never settle. There will be no prayers said over them, just like the people buried in the cemetery I showed you this morning. No one will mourn them because there will be no body to mourn over. They have disappeared." Nemat gripped the steering wheel tightly.

Carter knew enough about the language and culture that he had a pretty good idea what those men had done, and knowing just how close he and Nemat had come to meeting the same fate chilled him to the bone. If those men had shown up any earlier, he and Nemat might not have heard them or might not have been able to hide what they'd been doing.

"I know," Carter said. Nemat glanced over at him, and Carter was pretty sure Nemat knew what they'd just witnessed. "It's okay. Let's get back to your family. You will be safe there. I need to gather my things and try to figure out a way across the border into Turkey. Once I'm gone, you will be safe."

Nemat shook his head. "I will only be safe as long as I can change who I am."

"Nemat, you have to be careful. You cannot put yourself in danger," Carter said as his throat went as dry as the desert landscape outside the window. The thought of anything happening to Nemat made him crazy, as did the thought of him being with someone else. He knew he had no claim on the other man, but he couldn't stop the anger. He had no right, and Nemat deserved to be happy. The freedom Carter now saw that he had regardless of whether he'd told anyone about himself yet wasn't open to Nemat.

"I know that. I used to dream things would change here, that they could someday be like they are in Canada or the United States, but they never will be. We might topple the government and put a new one in place, but for me, and people like me, nothing will change." Nemat sounded depressed and forlorn. "I know that's the way it is, and I will have to live the rest of my life that way. My uncle will find me a wife, and I will do my best to make her happy. But I will never be happy."

"Nemat, I wish I could help, but I don't know what to say," Carter said.

"You do not have to say anything. You gave me happiness for a few hours. That is more than I ever expected. I know what my family would say, what my brother would do. They would most likely take me out and kill me the way those men did today."

"But they're your family," Carter told him.

"That's why they'd do it, to prevent me from sinning and shaming the family in the eyes of others and God." Nemat sighed. "I will not do anything when you go." Carter saw the compound appearing on the horizon. "Nothing more can happen between us while you stay with my uncle. But you gave me happiness, and I will always remember it. No matter what happens, I will always remember you."

Carter was speechless and blinked a few times, then wiped his eyes so Nemat wouldn't see he was on the verge of tears. The thought of Nemat being essentially alone for the rest of his life tore at him, but he had no idea what to do, or if there was anything that could be done. "I will always remember you too." Carter swallowed around the lump in his throat.

Nemat shook his head. "No, you must forget me. You must leave the country and tell your story. Get people to help us. You must find someone and be happy for both of us." Nemat slowed down and pulled into the compound. He drove the truck around the back and parked it out of sight. Then he led the way inside.

Carter knew the conversation was over. They had said all they could say on that subject. They would have no chance to talk privately, so Carter had to take what Nemat had said and hold it in his heart.

There was no one around, and Carter caught Nemat's eye for a second. He saw the pain and longing briefly, and then they were gone, hidden behind the wall Nemat had to put in place to protect himself both inside and out. Nemat turned away, and Carter closed his eyes, taking a deep breath before he went to the room he'd been given and closed the door.

For the past two days, he'd felt welcome in this house, but now he had to get away—out of this house and out of Syria. He needed to find a place where he could breathe and get some objective distance. He'd been developing feelings for Nemat for weeks, but up until a few days ago, those feelings were harmless. They'd been his and his alone. Now that he knew Nemat returned them, or at least was capable of returning them, he ached to be with him, but couldn't for both his safety and Nemat's. The best thing he could do was leave, and then Nemat could return to his life.

Carter went through his pack and made sure he had everything—all his notebooks, the flash drive, his phone… everything that documented all he'd seen and experienced. He would break a number of stories when he returned, and he had to be able to prove everything he said. He had little doubt the government would take interest in what he planned to report, and he needed everything, every detail, to be right.

A soft knock sounded on the door. Carter got up and opened it, then stepped back so Nasim could enter if he wished.

"Did you see?"

"Yes," Carter said, sure Nasim meant the cemetery. "I saw what I needed."

"Do you leave soon?" Nasim asked.

"Yes. Your hospitality has been wonderful," Carter said as he inclined his head slightly. "But I put you all in danger the longer I'm here, and I won't do that."

"Tomorrow Nemat will drive you close to the border. You mix with refugees, yes?"

Carter nodded, his stomach tightening with both nerves and excitement at the thought of being alone with Nemat again.

"We dress you like us and raise no suspicion," Nasim said.

"Thank you," Carter told him.

"You come smoke," Nasim said.

Carter realized it wasn't a question. He nodded again, and Nasim left. Carter closed the door and took a deep breath. Then he put on the robe that had been placed in the room for him and walked through the house. He found a number of men, mostly older, sitting around the pipe, as well as Nemat and Jalal. This time he didn't care what was in the pipe—he needed whatever oblivion he could get.

The men talked, and Carter understood very little. Some of the conversation was serious—from the tone, deadly serious—and he could guess at the topic. From the phrases he understood, they had to be talking about politics. Nemat was seated on the opposite side of the room, so Carter was on his own. He had no one to whisper the translation to him.

At one point, Nasim said something and the tone lightened. The men continued smoking and talking, but soon laughter filled the room. Food was brought, and they continued smoking, eating, and laughing. Carter had to give these people a great deal of credit. They could laugh and be happy at a time like this. It said a great deal about their spirit and sense of hope.

The day wore on and the sun set. Drinks and more food were brought, and they still sat and talked. Eventually Nemat stood and motioned to him, so Carter stood as well, acknowledging each person in the room before quietly taking his leave.

"We will leave just after sunrise," Nemat said. "I will drive you as close to the border as I dare. My plan is to pick up other refugees along the way. It will act as cover and allow you to blend in with the crowd."

"Thank you," Carter said, his throat constricting. "I need to get some rest, then." He went to his room, got his things, used the bathroom, cleaned up, and then returned to get ready for bed. He knew he wouldn't sleep well, and in fact was still awake staring into the dark hours later. He'd been in situations like this before. The best thing was to remain vigilant and not to panic. There would be many people trying to get out of Syria, and unless things had changed yet again, there would be people returning to Syria, so the border would be busy and chaotic. That should work well for him. Carter closed his eyes, and for the millionth time, he saw Nemat's face in his mind.

His door opened.

"Carter," Nemat whispered and slipped inside, then closed the door.

"I'm awake," he said and heard Nemat's light footsteps.

"I just had to say good-bye." Nemat leaned over the bed, and Carter felt his warm hands on his cheeks and then the lightest kiss on his lips. "I will not forget you."

"And I won't forget you," Carter said. It wasn't likely he would ever forget the first man he'd fallen in love with. He'd come to the other side of the world and snuck into a hostile country to get a story, but he'd gotten so very much more. Too bad he couldn't keep it, no matter how much he longed to. Nemat kissed him one more time and then stepped away. He silently left the room and closed the door behind him. Carter could still taste Nemat on his lips, but it was already fading. A few days, that was all they'd really had. How could he fall in love in just a few days? Carter tried his best to clear his mind, but couldn't. Eventually he fell asleep, but still he saw Nemat in his dreams.

CHAPTER THREE

CARTER WAS awake well before he heard movement in the house. He had his things packed and was dressed in an old robe and sandals that had been provided for him. He'd purposely not shaved for a couple of days. Thankfully, his beard came in dark to begin with. On close inspection there was no way he would pass for a native, but he was counting on no one looking too closely in the crowd of people he hoped to blend in with. By the time he heard a soft knock, he was ready to go. He opened the door and stepped out, then looked back into the room. "Please tell your family when you get back that I appreciate everything they've done. They will always be next to my own family in my heart."

"I will tell them," Nemat said, and then he turned and led him through the house and out to the old truck. They got in, and Nemat started the engine. They were about to pull away when Jalal appeared next to the truck and stuck his head through the open window.

"Be well," Jalal said. "We will not know if you make it, but we pray you get home safe and tell others what you have seen." He reached in and gripped Carter's wrist, and Carter gripped Jalal's in return. "I mean what I said. You are family. Honorable. Worthy." He gripped Carter's wrist tighter. "Good journey."

Carter smiled and wished Jalal well. Then they released each other's wrists. Jalal stepped back from the truck, and Nemat put the truck into gear and pulled away. Carter watched as Jalal got smaller in the distorted rearview mirror. Carter couldn't help wondering what Jalal would think or do if he knew how Carter felt about his brother and what the two of them had done.

"You will need papers once you get across the border," Nemat said.

"I have them. They're hidden on my body." Only a very close search would reveal them, and unless he was captured by the government, that kind of search wasn't likely. He hadn't bathed before he left and already felt dirty, but he needed to look as though he had been on the road and traveled some distance. That would help him blend in with the refugees. "I also have my notes and pictures."

Nemat nodded as they drove away from the compound. After a short ways, Nemat turned north and they headed toward the border. "This area is not controlled by the government, but no one is going to know you, so you must not trust anyone. Keep your head down, talk to no one, and blend in with the crowd as best you can."

Carter swallowed hard. "I will," he said. "And you do the same. Stay safe and look after Jalal when you go back to the city." He reached over and lightly squeezed Nemat's leg before pulling his hand back. He needed to touch him just one more time. He wanted to say he'd be back, but he couldn't make that promise. "I promise not to forget you."

"Will you write about me?" Nemat asked.

"Yes, though I will change your name to help keep you safe. But I will write about what I've seen and the people I've encountered. I will write about Syrian hospitality and heart. How they live life to the fullest and fight with all they have for a better life." Carter paused. "I'll write about all of you, and I'll write about what you've shown me." *Someday I'll be able to write about my feelings for you as well.*

Miles passed under the tires. Then they began to encounter refugees, some on foot, others piled in trucks. Nemat stopped to pick up a family, and they climbed in the back for the rest of the ride.

"The border is just a few miles," Nemat said as he pulled off the road. "I can take you farther, but I'm afraid someone might be desperate enough to try to take the truck from me."

Carter understood. He lifted his pack from the floor and reached to open the door. "You must get back to your family." He reached out and took Nemat's wrist the way his brother had done an hour or so earlier. "Stay safe," he whispered. The others got out of the back of the truck and joined the steady flow heading toward the border.

"Will you be back?" Nemat asked.

"I don't know. After I write my stories, I'll be a target for the government."

Nemat nodded. "You stay safe too." He swallowed. "I will not forget you and what you showed me."

"And I will not forget you," Carter said before he released Nemat's hand and stepped out of the truck. "Now, please turn around and go back to your family. I need to know that you'll be okay." Carter closed the door and stepped back. Nemat hesitated, and then Carter watched as the truck slowly began to move and turned around. He stood and watched as Nemat headed back the way they'd come. When he could no longer see the vehicle against the horizon, Carter turned and joined the others heading for the border.

As he walked, the number of people increased. He also encountered those heading the other way, back into Syria. It seemed as though there were huge numbers of people heading both ways in some mass indecisive migration. The closer he got to the border, the more chaotic things became, with carts, cars, and people on foot carrying all they had left of their lives. Carter made mental notes of everything he saw so he could use it in the story. He wished he could stop and speak to people, find out where they were from and what had happened to them, but it wasn't possible, and more than anything, he needed to get out.

At the border, Turkish soldiers stood guard, attempting to bring as much order as they could. Carter breathed a sigh of relief and looked for an opportunity to use the disorganization to his advantage. It didn't take him long. The crossing was so chaotic and loose that Carter slipped across hiding behind a truck. People jostled around him, everyone talking frantically. He didn't have to understand the language to hear the desperation and near panic in some of the voices. Others were calm and resigned. The people crossing the border were directed toward what Carter knew were refugee camps—places provided by the Turkish government and international aid agencies. These were tent cities that provided primitive basic services. Carter crested a small rise, and a sea of canvas spread out before him. No wonder people were returning to Syria. This wouldn't provide anyone with a sense of home or security for very long. Once the sound of the bombs faded and curiosity about loved ones became too great, they'd go back, like the people who had passed him on the road.

Carter stepped away from the group and fished out his phone. He hoped he could get a satellite signal. His luck held, and he dialed the number. "I'm out," he said when his editor, Kent, answered. He turned to look back across the border into Syria.

"Did you get plenty of material?" Kent asked.

"Yes. Enough to fuel things for quite a while and maybe set off an international firestorm," Carter said. "I just crossed the border, and I'm in Turkey. I'll try to get transportation to the nearest town. I'll send my GPS coordinates as soon as I hang up."

"Excellent," Kent said, and Carter imagined the gleam in his eye. "Did the contacts I gave you work out?" Kent had been a foreign correspondent in Syria earlier in his career, and he'd provided Carter with some contacts he felt were still viable. One of those contacts had gotten Carter in touch with Nemat and Jalal's band. He knew people who knew people.

"Yes. He was able to get me with a band of fighters," Carter explained. "I've got to go. I need to keep moving."

"I'll get transportation arranged," Kent said and then hung up. Carter texted the coordinates and waited for a reply that they'd been received before moving on.

He was out. The nervousness that had been present with him for the entire time he was in Syria fell away, replaced with excitement about the work ahead. He had places to get to and stories to write. But first he had to get to a town and then to Istanbul, where he could pick up the equipment he'd left in safekeeping. Then he could fly home. Carter pulled a container of water out of his weathered pack, drained it, and then hoisted the pack back onto his back before heading off in the direction of the nearest town.

HIS PLANE lifted off from the airport in Istanbul two days later.
That was the earliest flight he could get. In that time, Carter had
written two intensely powerful stories and was working on a third.
Each time he filed a story and sent it to Kent, he got a return call
filled with something he didn't think was possible from the seasoned
news veteran: glee. During those days he hadn't had time to think of
anything other than his writing and making sure he could prove each
part of his story with facts he'd gathered. He'd also sent pictures to
back up what he'd written, including the one with the arm he'd dug
up. He hadn't included the GPS coordinates in the story, but he had
sent them to Kent as part of his proof.

As the plane gained altitude, an announcement was made that
electronic devices could be used again. Carter pulled his computer
out of the bag and turned it on, then immediately began to write. The
one story he had yet to compose was the one about the band of men.
He'd decided to tell Nemat's story as a freedom fighter—the
conflict through the eyes of a young man with promise. After
working for two hours, he had very little he was happy with. The
story was coming off flat and lifeless. This type of story had to have
impact. His computer began flashing messages that his battery was
dangerously low, so he shut it down and leaned back in his seat,
closing his eyes.

He immediately thought of Nemat, wondering if he'd gotten
home okay, if he was all right, and if he and his brother had returned
to the city to fight once again. Carter pulled up his phone and
flipped through the photographs until he came to the picture he'd
taken of Nemat in Aleppo. He'd looked at that picture so many
times, if it had been a printed photograph, it would already be
creased and worn. With a sigh, he closed the photo application and
stuffed the phone back into his pocket.

Carter tried to sleep, but was restless despite his fatigue. For
the past few days, he'd woken each night at least once to the sound
of gunfire that wasn't actually there. He'd calmed himself and gone
back to sleep each time, but he found the phenomenon disturbing.
He knew he hadn't been in a combat zone long enough to

experience PTSD. This had happened before, though, and he hoped it would pass like it had the previous times. He closed his eyes again and must have drifted off because suddenly he was with Nemat. They were in the house in the desert, except this time, the men pulled Nemat outside, and a few seconds later shots rang out like they had that day. He woke with a gasp and looked around. A few people had turned his way, but they quickly went back to what they were doing, and Carter tried to still his pounding heart. This was for the best. Nemat was safer now that he was gone. Carter unfastened his seat belt and walked down the aisle to the bathroom. Once inside, he locked the door and held his head in his hands. Then he did something his mother would be proud of—he closed his eyes and prayed.

Carter returned to his seat after splashing a little water on his face. He settled in as best he could and eventually fell asleep out of sheer exhaustion. He woke when the cabin crew brought food, and then he prepared for landing in London. He had hours before his next flight and managed to find a place to plug in. He spent much of the time sitting in one of the chairs struggling with how to write the story he wanted to tell. Eventually he gave up and worked on something different so he'd have something fresh to present when he arrived. His plane was on time and he boarded. They took off for New York and home base, and Carter continued working once he could use his laptop, managing to finish his story about the state of Aleppo and what had become of the city and its inhabitants just before his battery ran out.

By the time he landed, Carter's legs and back ached, his butt hurt from sitting, and he could barely keep his eyes open. He called Kent and told him about the story he was sending over, then said, "I'm going to the apartment to rest."

"Good, good," Kent told him. "Get some rest. We'll see you in the morning, and we can figure out how to handle the explosive fallout your mass grave story is going to generate when it hits the streets in a few hours. I suspect you'll be asked for interviews and the like."

Carter sighed. "If I am, turn them all down. I can only do my job if people don't know my face."

"Kid," Kent said and then paused. "This could make your career, catapult you into the realm of the big fish. Are you sure you want to turn it down? Think about it, and we'll talk in the morning." Kent disconnected the call, and Carter flipped through his contacts and made another call.

"Hi, Mom, it's me," he said when his mother answered the phone. "I just landed in New York."

"Thank God. I've been worried sick since you went to that godforsaken country." He knew part of her reaction was relief that he was back in the country and safe, so he let the remark go. "Will you be able to come to visit soon?" His parents lived in Central Pennsylvania, outside Harrisburg. It was a four-hour train ride, but right now all he could think about was staying in one place for a while. He knew that might not be possible, but he hoped for a little time between foreign assignments.

"Maybe. I have more material to write, and I'm going to be busy for a while. There are going to be a lot of stories coming out in the next few days. You won't hear my name, but a lot of them will be because of me." Carter couldn't help letting a hint of pride slide into his voice.

"Okay, honey," she said and then proceeded to catch him up on all the news. "Your sister told us last night that she's pregnant again."

"Mom, don't you think she should share that news?" Carter asked.

"Just act surprised when she tells you," his mother said. Then she described her aches and pains, his father's latest diabetic scare, and what was going on at the church. It was like he'd never left, and somehow that was comforting. He wondered how long that comfortable feeling would last. On the plane, he'd had time to think, once his laptop battery life had ended, and he'd decided it was time to be honest with his family. They deserved to know the truth. He'd kept who he was hidden for so long—too long, he'd realized. He half listened to what she was saying, then finally interrupted her to say, "I need to get through customs and get some rest. I'll call you soon." They said their good-byes, and Carter descended the stairs and got in line at immigration.

It took a while to get his passport stamped. Of course he was flagged and sent for additional screening by customs, because that was just his luck. By the time he was done, Carter was so tired he could barely move. He stood in line for a cab and then rode downtown to his apartment. He paid the driver and carried his things up the stairs and inside the building.

The apartment was stuffy, so he opened a window to let in the fresh air. He had no food in the house at all. The refrigerator had been shut off with the door left open. Carter called for delivery, made up the bed, showered quickly, and answered the door in sleep pants and a T-shirt. He paid the deliveryman, tipping him well, and then sat on the sofa to eat. By the time he was done, Carter was winded. He threw away the trash, pulled the curtains, and collapsed onto the bed, falling asleep before he knew it.

A loud, incongruous noise woke him. Carter groaned and cracked his eyes open. It was completely dark in the room. He glanced at the clock, which showed it was just after ten. The sound came again, and he reached for his landline telephone. "Hello," he said.

"Oh my God!" he heard his friend Joan scream into the phone. "I've been calling every day for two weeks. I was beginning to think you were dead."

"Hi, Joan," Carter said, smiling despite himself.

"When did you get in? Why didn't you call? You know I'm never going to forgive you for not calling and telling me you were alive. Okay, yes, I will, but only if you tell me everything."

"Joan, breathe," Carter said, but she barely paused.

"I'm on my way over right now, and I'll get stuff for dinner. You can eat, right?" Joan asked, and Carter imagined her getting ready to leave her place as she talked. "I'll be there as soon as I get the food. Is Chinese okay? Of course it is; you love Chinese." He heard a door close in the background. "So, did you meet interesting people?"

"Joan, hon, why don't you hang up, get the food, and let me get dressed so I don't answer the door wearing only a smile. Okay?"

She laughed heartily. "Okay. I don't want to see your bits and pieces, so get dressed and I'll see you soon." She hung up, and Carter got out of bed. He dressed and left his tiny bedroom. He sat in the living area and turned on the television, watching nothing in particular until the buzzer sounded. He let Joan in the building, unlocked his door, and waited for her to come up. She must have run up the stairs because the door opened seconds later. She placed the food on the counter, hurried over to him, and threw her arms around his neck, squealing in his ear. "God, I'm glad you're back." She rocked him back and forth as she hugged him before stepping back and then hugging him again. "So was it as bad as you thought?"

"It was worse than I could have ever imagined," Carter said. "And yet in some ways it was wondrous. These people fight for what they believe in and then go home and are able to laugh and live their lives. It blew me away."

Joan rushed to the counter, brought over the food and drinks, and placed them on the coffee table. "So did you get the stories you were looking for?" She pulled out small containers of food and handed one to him.

"Yes," Carter answered as he opened the container, his stomach rumbling. "I got some amazing stories that I've already filed, and there are more I have yet to write." Joan handed him a fork, and he dug in. "I still have to write the hardest story." Carter reached for his phone and pulled up his pictures. The photos for the stories had been transferred to the office computers, so all he had left on the phone now were the innocuous ones. "This used to be a thriving city and now it's a war zone." He turned the phone to show her ruined buildings and smoke rising into the air from various buildings. "You can see it used to be beautiful and incredibly vibrant. Now both sides fight building to building, measuring success in blocks or even houses." He changed the picture.

"Who's that?" Joan asked, grabbing the phone. He took it back and glanced at the photograph of Nemat before changing it.

"These are the fighters I spent most of my time with. They looked out for each other and for me," Carter said. "They were an incredible group of men. They saved my life more than once, and I was able to save one of theirs." Carter continued eating. "It's their story I'm having a tough time telling. I decided to write about one of them, but it comes off too sterile and without drama."

Joan took the phone. "Is the story about him?" she asked, indicating Nemat's image. Carter nodded and went back to eating. Joan looked at him and then back at the picture. She showed it to him again, and Carter smiled briefly before returning to his food.

"I wanted to tell the story of the fighters through one of them," Carter said. "I can't use his real name because it will put him in danger, but I need to tell the story. I'm just at a loss to figure out how to do it right."

Joan sifted through the other photos, but kept going back to the one of Nemat. "Was he looking at you when you snapped this?"

"Yeah, I guess so. We were busy at the time, and I only had a few seconds. Why?" Carter asked.

Joan set the phone down and picked up her Mongolian beef. It was what she always got. "No reason," she said, and Carter stifled a groan. Those two words meant she thought she was on to something. "How long are you back for?"

"I wish I knew. I should be here for a few weeks. I need to go to the doctor tomorrow and get checked out. I've also got a number of stories to write." Something on the television caught his attention, and he turned up the volume.

"The Syrian government has announced a major offensive around the city of Aleppo. They claim to be making ground and routing out the bands they claim are terrorists. The White House reports that the president and his advisors are meeting to determine the United States's response." The story moved on, and Carter set down his food.

"That's where they're fighting," he whispered.

"There's nothing you can do," Joan said.

"Except write my stories and hope they're powerful enough to get someone to help them," Carter told her. "I promised I'd do my best."

Joan scoffed. "If I know you, and I do, you turned in great stories before you got on the plane and wrote more once you landed.

I know this last story has you stymied, but give it a little time." She continued eating. "So, tell me what Syria is like."

"Hot," Carter quipped. "It was once a beautiful country. But now so much of it has been destroyed. Some parts are still nice, but areas that have been fought over have been destroyed. Landmarks that had been there for hundreds of years are gone, reduced to piles of rubble." Carter picked up his cashew chicken and slowly began to eat. "I'm not naïve enough to say that the government is to blame for all of it, but it's a shame." Carter thought of the other things he'd seen, the atrocities of war. Joan didn't need to hear about those.

"So, did you get close to the guy in the photo?" Joan asked. He should have known she'd let it go too easily earlier.

"Yes. Nemat and Jalal said I was family because I had saved Nemat's life. When they left the battle, I went with them to their family's compound." Carter picked up his phone. "They were welcoming, and the hospitality was amazing. They shared what they had, and when you consider that they would all be in danger if I was discovered there by the government, it was pretty unbelievable."

"So, you were in danger?" Joan asked.

"The entire time I was in the country. I've never felt that way before. I'd been in war zones in other countries, but always with US troops or in reasonably secure areas. This time I was on my own, and it was exhilarating." Carter finished up his food and set the container aside. "There's something I need to tell you."

Joan set down her food and gave him her full attention. "What is it?"

"When I was over there, some things became very clear to me. You and I have been friends for four years, and you know you have to drag things out of me." Joan rolled her eyes. They'd met when Joan had been Kent's administrative assistant. Joan had gotten a better job and moved on a few years ago, but their friendship had been set. She'd often said he was like a locked safe with a small hole in it that allowed a nugget of information to escape once in a blue moon. "Well, I realized how precious life is when I was there." Carter swallowed. "I saw people die, and I don't want that to happen to me without people knowing who I really am." Carter shifted in his seat. "I've kept quiet about myself because of the job and my family for so long it's become a habit." Carter sipped from his bottle of water. "I'm gay." He waited for her reaction.

Joan made a rolling motion with her fingers, and Carter stared at her. "That's it? You have this big epiphany, and all I get is that you're gay? Please, I've known you were gay for years." She reached over and lightly slapped him on the arm. "Duh...."

"Joan...."

"Come on." She shoved out her chest. "Every guy I meet looks at my tits first and my eyes second, because, let's face it, I've got a great rack. But you never did. It became obvious to me that you were most likely gay a few months after we met." Joan became serious. "At first I had this notion that you were boyfriend material, but we just became friends instead. And after a while, we settled into the relationship we have."

Carter was shocked. He stared at her, openmouthed. Here he'd made this big announcement, and she'd treated it like it was no big deal. "That's it?"

"Honey," Joan said as she jumped up and hugged the stuffing out of him, "I'm happy you feel comfortable enough to tell me. I know that's a huge step." She hugged him again and then sat back down. "Does this mean I can start fixing you up?" She rubbed her hands together gleefully. "I know so many guys who would die to go out with a hottie like you." She bounced with excitement.

"Joan, let's not go off the deep end," Carter told her. He glanced at his phone and sighed softly. "Let me try to meet people on my own first before you call in the big guns, okay?"

"Fine," she said, rolling her eyes. "Do you have any idea how long I've waited for you to say something?"

"Then why didn't *you* say something?" Carter asked.

"Because this is one of those things that had to come from you," Joan told him seriously. "If I'd been wrong, then I'd have run the risk of hurting you, and if you weren't ready, you'd have denied it anyway and pulled into your shell." She picked up her beef and ate a few more bites before standing up and throwing away the containers. While she was in the kitchen, she opened the refrigerator. "Good Lord," she said, turning toward him. "If I hadn't called, you'd have starved to death."

"I just got in this morning—give me a break. I'm supposed to go into the office tomorrow. Kent is so excited to learn what else I have." He turned back to the television to see if there was anything else in the news, but they seemed to be running the same thing over and over. Carter turned it off. "The first story should be printing as we speak and will hit the newsstands in the morning. This should really give us a boost." Carter sat back and relaxed, truly relaxed, for the first time in weeks. "It should create quite a stir."

"Can you tell me about it?" Joan asked.

"Nope. It's way too hot." With Facebook and other social media, a story could spread faster than the paper could publish, so the only way to ensure a scoop was to keep his mouth shut, even with friends.

"Can I tell people you're back?" she asked.

"Of course. My mother is already spreading the word."

Joan gasped. "Do your parents know? About you being gay, I mean."

"No. I'm trying to figure out how to tell them," Carter said. "The way I figure it, they'll probably freak and end up on my doorstep within hours to try and save me."

"Come on. Your folks love you, and they aren't as backward as you like to make them out to be. Yes, it's going to be hard for them, but probably because you've kept it from them for so long." She paused. "Are you going to tell anyone at work?"

"No. Some of my assignments are in sensitive areas, and I don't want that compromised." The truth was a lot of his foreign work had been in the Middle East, and he didn't want his sexuality to affect his ability to do his job. He wasn't sure how the paper would react, and he didn't want to find out. "Are there any more questions? I thought I was the reporter."

"Just one," Joan said and grabbed his phone. Thankfully it had gone to sleep and she didn't have the password. "Is the guy in the picture someone special?" She leaned forward, waiting for him to answer. "Is that why you're having trouble writing the story?"

"I don't know what he is or how I feel about him," Carter answered honestly. "And I'm not sure if that's why I'm having trouble with the story, or if I simply need a little distance."

"From the story, or from him?" Joan asked. Damn, the woman could zero in on an issue sometimes, and she'd hit the bull's-eye. The thing was, he wasn't sure what the correct answer was. "Honey, I'm going to go and let you rest. You're still tired, and they'll expect to see you at the paper bright and early tomorrow." She stood up and hugged him gently, then kissed his cheek. "Call me tomorrow and let me know what happens, and I'll pick up a copy of the paper to see this big story." She smiled and left the apartment.

After a few minutes, Carter turned the television on again. He watched the news for a little while to see if there was anything new. There wasn't. Then he turned it off, checked that the apartment door was locked, and went to bed. He didn't fall asleep right away, and thought about how easy it had been to tell Joan about himself. He hoped telling others would be as easy, but he wasn't counting on it. Eventually he closed his eyes and sleep overtook him. In the morning, he woke, not remembering if he'd dreamed, but a calm, warm feeling permeated him nonetheless.

THE NEWSROOM was hopping when he got into the office. He sat at his desk and checked his e-mail, hoping to have five minutes of quiet. It wasn't to be. Other staff members came in, and all of them stopped by his desk to pat him on the back.

"Carter," Kent called from his office, a smile on his usually grumpy face. Once Carter had stepped inside, Kent closed the door. "Everyone has picked up on your story about the mass grave. The television media is reporting it and citing us as the source. The other stories are set to run as well. We've had calls from various government agencies, and they'd like to speak with you. It seems we've scooped everyone, including the CIA." Kent looked almost giddy. "Our lawyers will be with you when you meet with them, and we've decided to give them no more than what we printed." Kent walked around and sat at his desk. "I'm assuming you have more."

"We have the GPS coordinates for the cemetery that I sent you. I didn't dig around much, so I don't know how big it is, but as I wrote in the story, what I uncovered took only three shovels full of dirt. The desert wind could be uncovering the remains as we speak," Carter explained.

"We'll talk to the lawyers about giving them the coordinates, but after that, the information is all ours. How much more material is there?" Kent asked. Carter could see him trying to milk this for weeks.

"I have three in-depth pieces planned about the life of a Syrian freedom fighter." Carter sighed. "As well as at least two on life in and out of the war zone. But it's the story that got away that's bothering me." Carter leaned forward and told Kent about the incident in the abandoned mansion. "I know in my heart why those men were executed, but I can't prove it and wasn't able to get any additional proof for fear the men would return."

The news didn't seem to faze Kent in the least. "You go ahead and write your stories. I want to feature them on a daily basis. Our firsthand Syrian reporter is home, and we need to make the most of it. Who knows? The columns are certain to get picked up by the wire services, and that will mean even more exposure."

"That's good," Carter said with a smile. "Was there anything else you wanted?"

"Not right now. Welcome home." He extended his hand, and Carter shook it. "Now get back to work."

Carter left the office and closed the door. One of the guys in the room turned up one of the television monitors. "The *New York Press* is reporting the discovery of a mass grave in Syria. One of their reporters unearthed it while deeply undercover in that country." The room broke into applause, drowning out the rest of the story. Carter smiled and walked back toward his desk, grinning. Once he reached it, he sat down, checked his e-mail again, and then got back to work. Regardless of the applause and his story being featured on television, he still had a deadline he had to meet and stories Kent wanted polished.

He worked for two hours on the first of his pieces about the life of a freedom fighter. He thought about using some of the pictures he'd taken, but that would only put the people who'd helped him in danger. So instead, he paired the story with photos of the destruction being caused. He had a few pictures that didn't show faces, so he included those as well. He figured the Syrian government was going to discover any information he printed. Late in the morning, he sent his story to Kent. After breathing a sigh of relief, he then organized the rest of his material for the remaining two articles. He ate at his desk and had started work on his next story when all hell broke loose. The newspaper's central systems began going down. Carter saved all his material to his flash drive and then detached it before shutting down his desktop. "We're being hacked," Kent called. "Secure all material." Kent rushed over to Carter's desk. "Where are your notes and source material?"

Carter grinned and patted his backpack. "It's all safe. Why? Do you think that's what they're looking for?"

"Our people are still working on it. But it seems suspicious that we're being attacked just after your story broke." Kent hurried through the newsroom while Carter gathered his things. He was ready to go home, but stayed around in case this did indeed have anything to do with his story. He sat back down and waited a little longer.

"Kent, do we know anything?" Carter asked as his boss breezed through the room.

"Not really. They don't know where it was coming from yet. The systems are coming back up, and they believe they've repaired the security hole that was exploited." Kent walked toward his office, and Carter followed and dropped into one of the chairs.

"Aside from the stories themselves, none of my stuff is in the system," Carter explained.

"That's good, but there hadn't been enough time for anyone to get something like this together and have it be about you," Kent told him. "We've had things like this happen before. No one has ever gotten this far into our systems before, though." He sounded more than a little worried. "Go on home. You've done great work, and I know there will be more."

"Thanks," Carter said and grabbed his things before taking the elevator down to the ground floor and leaving the building. He'd always loved the city. He headed right home, dropped off his things, and headed out again. He needed to get some things in the apartment, but found he needed to walk and be outside even more. He just walked, block after block, looking up and ahead. A couple walked in front of him for a few blocks, two men whose hands brushed every once in a while. They were so obviously together and cared for each other. Carter saw how they looked at one another every now and then. As he did, he glanced at the empty space beside him and wondered what it would be like to be able to show his city to someone he cared for. Almost instantly he found himself wondering what Nemat would think of New York. Would he be impressed or scared? Carter liked to think he'd be impressed, or at least curious.

Carter sighed and continued walking. He'd never wondered before how he could live in a city with millions of people, dozens of them right around him almost all the time, and yet spend much of his time alone. His phone vibrated in his pocket, and he pulled it out, checked the screen, and answered it. "Hi, Mom."

"You sound down," she said right away. "Are you eating enough?"

"Mom," Carter groaned. "Actually, I'm tired."

"Then tell that boss of yours you need a few days off and come for a visit. Hop on the train. You can work from here and send in your stories. You can even bring Joan with you. She's so nice." His mother had been pushing him and Joan together ever since her last visit. Joan had taken his mother on a shopping tour. She and his mother had hit it off, and now his mother was determined that Joan would make the perfect daughter-in-law.

"She has to work, but yeah, I think I'll come for a visit." Carter reminded himself to speak to Kent about it. "I'll call you tomorrow and let you know when."

"Good," his mother said excitedly. "It's been so long, and I was worried about you every day you were gone. I know you couldn't call, but it was hard not knowing if you were alive." She sniffed slightly. "I kept watching the news for stories that you might have been caught or killed." He didn't tell her it wasn't likely anyone would hear if either happened. The most likely scenario was that he'd simply disappear.

He talked to her for a while as he walked to the doctor's office. He ended the call as he arrived, and after a thorough checkup, he left and stopped at the store on his way home, where he stocked up on all the groceries he could carry. Then, as night fell and the streetlights came on, he turned down his street and entered his building, then climbed the stairs to his place.

Inside, he put all the stuff away and booted up his laptop. Then he got down to work. Things were flowing for him. The block he'd experienced just the day before had disappeared, and the story he wanted to tell flowed from his mind to his hands and onto the screen. His phone vibrated, but he ignored it. He tossed the phone on one of the cushions to silence the noise, then kept on working. Everything was going perfectly, and within a few hours he had finished the story. He saved it and made a backup copy out of habit before closing his laptop for the evening.

His front door buzzer sounded as he was about to make something to eat. He called down to find out who it was.

"Carter, it's Joan. Let me in," she said frantically. He buzzed her in and waited until she nearly burst into the apartment. "I figured you'd be working." She picked up the remote and turned on the television, then found one of the news stations.

"Our top story this evening: reports out of Syria on the possible use of chemical weapons in remote areas of the country. The government is blaming the attacks on the rebels, but a Pentagon spokesman said that it's unlikely the rebel groups possess that technology. Any chemical-weapons attack is most likely the government testing the resolve of the US and other nations." A map of Syria flashed on the screen and then zoomed in. Carter gasped when the map narrowed in on the area of the country where Nemat and his family lived. "Reports are that the attacks happened east of Aleppo in an area of the country largely out of government control. The release appears to be limited and might be a test."

Carter continued staring at the screen even after the story ended. "That's where Nemat and his family are," he said softly. He swallowed hard and tried not to worry. He had no way to contact them. Hell, he might never know if they were all right, if Nemat was safe, and he had to learn to live with that.

CHAPTER
FOUR

"THIS CONVERSATION is strictly off the record," the agent said sternly.

The following day, Carter and Kent sat across the table from two government agents. They had refused to say which agency they were with, even though Kent had asked repeatedly, and they'd asked questions Carter either couldn't or wouldn't answer.

"My client has no obligation to speak to you at all," the newspaper's lawyer said. The man was steely-eyed and as cool as a cucumber, which Carter found reassuring. "I advise you refrain from answering any of their questions," he told Carter.

"As I said, I will not provide you with the names of anyone I spoke with. They are my sources and must be protected. You know that," Carter told both agents and saw the first hint of respect from them. Carter turned to the lawyer and then back to the agents. Then he reached into his pocket, extracted a piece of paper, and slid it across the table. "This is what I can provide you."

The agent in charge, who'd said his name was Dempsey, took the paper. He unfolded it. "GPS coordinates," he said, showing it to Agent Reynolds, who said nothing.

"Yes. I got them off my phone at the location where I found the body. I can't say how many are there, but my guide told me to dig anywhere." Carter sat back and folded his hands over his chest. "I'm doing this because I hope you'll be able to help my friends."

Agent Dempsey leaned across the table. "You sound like you developed some sympathy for the rebels when you were there. Did you meet anyone from the Syrian government?"

"I have told you what I will tell you," Carter said.

"You traveled into a country hostile to the United States. That alone is suspicious," Dempsey began.

Carter smiled slightly. "Knock off the cloak-and-dagger crap. This isn't the McCarthy era. You can be as paranoid as you like." He leaned forward, meeting Dempsey's gaze. "Under the First Amendment, I can tell you what you can do with your bullying and threats. I can also write an excellent story about being coerced by the CIA. I bet that would make great news coverage. I've cooperated as best I can with you. I truly hope it's a help and that you can do something for the people fighting for some of the same freedoms you profess to protect." Carter stood up. "Thank you for coming. As agreed up front, I will not use any of our conversation, but any follow-up or further interactions will be considered on the record."

The agents looked at each other before standing up. Carter extended his hand, and to his surprise they both shook it. He took that as a hopeful sign.

"Should you decide to make another foray to contact your sources, we might be able to provide assistance. Off the record, of course." Dempsey handed Carter a card with a phone number on it and nothing else. Then the agents turned and left the room. Kent stood up and closed the door.

"Kid, you've got cojones," the lawyer told Carter.

"He's one of my best," Kent said. "I think you're done for the rest of the week. Your stories are in and set to run. Take the time you requested with your family. I don't want to see you until Monday." Kent smiled, and Carter sighed softly. Out of the frying pan and into the fire, so to speak. He stood up and shook hands with the lawyer and Kent before leaving the conference room. He stopped to grab his things at his desk, shut down his computer, and headed out before anyone could stop him.

Carter strode out of the building and hailed a cab. At home, he packed hurriedly while he called his mother and told her he was leaving a little earlier than he planned. Then he went online and bought his train tickets. In less than an hour, he was packed and out the door, hailing another cab to take him to Penn Station. Carter called Joan from the train station and told her he was going to see his family. Once his train was called, he descended the stairs and found a seat on the nearly full train, then settled in for the four-hour ride to Harrisburg.

He tried to rest and relax on the journey, but nervousness around the news he'd decided to tell his parents kept him awake for the entire trip. At Philadelphia, there was an engine change, so he hurried up into the 30th Street station and got some food, then returned to his seat to eat.

For the final leg of his journey, he plugged in his laptop and spent much of the trip playing games or mindlessly surfing the Internet. About an hour out of Harrisburg, he called his mother and told her the train would be on time. She sounded excited, and truthfully, he was as well. While overseas, he'd been completely cut off from the outside world. More than once he'd wondered if his parents were okay, and he could only imagine what they'd gone through worrying about him.

The train pulled to a stop, and he gathered his suitcase, laptop bag, and coat before lugging everything off the train and up the stairs to the station. As soon as he stepped inside and got out of the flow of traffic, he heard his mother gasp. He put down his bags, and she hugged him within an inch of his life. She stepped back and said, "You're so thin," and then she hugged him again.

"Mom, there are people starving where I was," he whispered to her. She ignored him, rocking slightly, and burst into tears. His father looked shaken as well, and once she released him, it was his father's turn.

"The car is parked right out front," he said, and he led the way through the station to a silver Focus. Carter put his things in the trunk and got in the backseat.

Carter closed his eyes as his father pulled out. His mother started talking, but she quieted after a minute. "Have you slept much?" she asked him.

"No," Carter answered. His mind wouldn't let him rest. He had too many deadlines, too many stories that needed to be told. He'd finally gotten the urgent ones written, and now he was going to concentrate on a few in-depth stories that would require more thought and time. He hoped he would get that time at home, along with some much-needed rest. "I'll be okay now."

"Of course you will. You're home," his mother said. Carter hummed and closed his eyes once again as his father veered onto the freeway on-ramp. "We were so worried."

"I know, Mom," he said. "But I did what I had to do. I'm glad I did."

"Was it as dangerous as they say on television?"

"Yes. It's a war zone, and it was even more dangerous for me because I wasn't supposed to be there," Carter said. "I had to be on my toes all the time. But I met some good people, and they helped watch my back while I watched theirs." He paused, and the conversation halted for a while.

"It's a shame that lovely girl couldn't come with you."

"Mom," Carter groaned.

"You need to find a nice girl and settle down," she said.

He stifled another groan, but said nothing. This was not the time to break the news that there would never be a nice girl for him. Most definitely not in the car. Visions of fiery vehicular death passed through his head. "Mom, let's not talk about that, at least until we get home." If he could put off that particular conversation for a day or two, he'd be happy.

"Leave him alone," his father said from the driver's seat. "He's home and in one piece. Let that be enough for now." That seemed to satisfy his mother, and they rode in relative peace and quiet the rest of the way.

The ride from the train station to the hundred-year-old Georgian Revival home he'd grown up in was only twenty minutes. Once they'd parked out front, Carter got out. His father popped the trunk, and Carter got his bags. As he approached the house, the front door opened and his two-and-a-half-year-old nephew, Dean, flew out toward him.

"Uncle Carter," he squealed.

Carter set down his bags and scooped Dean into his arms. He spun around, and the little boy giggled. "How are you, bud?" he asked before running him around the yard. "Did you miss me?"

"Yes," he said, and then he giggled. "Mama has a baby growing in her belly."

"That was supposed to be a secret," Carter's sister Catherine said as she approached. Carter put Dean down and hugged her tight. "I'm glad you're back. We were all worried sick."

"I know, Cat," Carter said. "I missed you all too." Dean tugged on his pants, and Carter let go of Cat before picking him up. "Let's go inside."

"I'm hungry," Dean announced. "Gramma, can I have a apple?" His mother had never had candy of any kind in the house when they'd been growing up, and it looked like she hadn't varied from that now that she had a grandchild. He and Cat had been taking bets that she'd cave once Dean was born, but it didn't look like it.

"I'm going to make dinner," his mother told Dean. "Can you wait a little while like a big boy?"

Dean looked around. "Okay. But not too long," he answered and then squirmed to get down. As soon as Carter set him on his feet, he ran inside the house.

"He doesn't walk anywhere," Cat said. "He runs." She sounded tired.

"Are you okay?" Carter asked her.

"Yes, being pregnant and keeping up with him is wearing me out. Phillip is out on a job and won't be home for a few weeks. I can manage, but it's hard. Mom keeps Dean a day a week, and that helps, but on the other days it's all I can do to get him in bed and not collapse." She sighed. "I've been looking into day care, but the cost is too much when we're living on the one income."

"Maybe Dean and I can do some guy things one day while I'm here," Carter offered.

"Oh gosh, bless you," she said. "All I really want is an hour to myself so I can take a shower."

Carter sniffed loudly, and she smacked him for it. "Don't worry about it. I can take him to the park and let him play it all out.

But not today." He hoisted his bag and walked inside. He carried his bags up to his old room, which had been redone as the guest room, but it was comfortable, and he didn't expect or want his mother to keep his old things. He set down his stuff on the floor and sighed loudly before sitting on the edge of the bed. Then he kicked off his shoes and lay down, closing his eyes, letting the comfort of home wash over him.

AFTER CATCHING a brief nap and eating until he thought he'd burst, Carter sat on the front porch in one of the old wicker chairs his mother had bought when he was a teenager. She painted them every few years, and they were nearly as clean as the day she brought them home.

"Is something bothering you?" Cat asked as she stepped out into the cool autumn air, closing the door behind her. "You seem different."

"I guess I am," he said softly.

"I guess you saw stuff none of us can understand," she said, sitting in one of the other chairs. "Mom is putting Dean to bed. She and Dad are up there reading him a story just like they used to do for us." She paused for a few seconds. "You know you can talk to me."

Carter thought for a second. "Are you sure?" he asked softly. "Things have changed, but I don't know if you're ready to hear about them."

"Why don't you try me?" she asked. Cat had never backed down from a fight in her life. That was how she'd met Phillip. He'd made a pass at her. She'd reportedly slapped him, not once, but twice, and then dared him to act like a gentleman. He had from that day on, at least according to her.

"Well, I saw a number of things, people killing each other, fighting over a few blocks back and forth for days on end. I saw how fragile life is." He paused the rocking chair. "And I realized some things. Life is too short to hide or pull punches." He pulled out his phone, and she moved closer so she could see. "These are the men I fought with. That's Jalal, Hassan, Ashur, and the other men." He flipped the photograph.

"Who's that?"

"His name's Nemat," Carter answered. "He's Jalal's brother."

He lifted his gaze in time to see Cat shudder. "That's a powerful image. What's he looking at?"

"I wasn't sure at first, but I know now—he was looking at me," Carter answered.

Cat took the phone from him and stared at it. "Do you have something to tell me?" she asked. "Because this image says a lot more than I think either of you meant to say." Cat lifted her gaze and handed the phone back to him. She sat back, obviously waiting.

"What do you want me to say?" Carter asked.

"How about the truth," Cat countered.

"You want me to tell you that I'm gay?" he challenged.

Cat shrugged, and Carter wondered why everyone he told kept doing that. "See? Was that so hard?" She smiled at him.

"You knew?" he asked.

"Not really. I always thought you were busy, and Mom kept talking about this girl you were seeing. But I don't give a rat's ass. It's not that big a thing anymore. Kids at the school I used to volunteer at in town are coming out at fourteen. It's going to be hard on Mom and Dad, though."

"I know. But at least you're giving them grandchildren, so that pressure's off me," Carter told her flippantly.

"So, does he"—she pointed toward the phone—"have anything to do with this?"

"I guess so. He has to lie for the rest of his life or risk being killed, most likely by his own family to preserve their honor and to keep him from sinning," Carter said. "It was very hard leaving him behind. I didn't have a choice, and I doubt he could leave his family. They're everything to him." Carter inhaled and then released his breath slowly.

"Do you know what you feel for him?" Cat asked, and it was his turn to shrug.

"Doesn't really matter—it isn't as though I can simply go back. I'm probably already wanted by the Syrian government. By now they'll have seen the articles and know I was in the country. They're probably fit to be tied over the mass grave story. Trying to get back inside the country would be more hazardous than anyone can believe."

"How can they stop anyone? The place is a mess. There have to be people coming and going all the time. I watch the news. There are parts of the country they don't control. Cross there." Everything was so practical for her.

"I wish it were that simple. Even the other side can be dangerous. Trust me." He suppressed a shudder as he thought about the executions by the house. "In war, no one is truly innocent."

Cat nodded slowly. "So, how long have you known that you were gay?" she whispered, looking toward the door.

"A long time," Carter said and sighed again. "This is really uncomfortable. I guess I've known since I was a teenager, but didn't want to deal with who I was. I figured I wouldn't be able to do the job I wanted, and you know how Mom and Dad feel. They're wonderful, and I love them both to death, but what if they turn their back on me? Mom spends her extra time at the church, and I remember the sermons from when we were kids. They were so vitriolic, and Mom dragged us there every Sunday."

"I think Mom and Dad will surprise you," Cat told him.

"I hope so, but it still doesn't stop the worry from deep in my gut," Carter said. "My entire life could change because of telling Mom and Dad."

Cat shook her head. "Your life has already changed. What Mom and Dad think isn't going to change much. You already know what you believe. Heck, you survived a war zone in a foreign country when you were on your own. This is nothing. Mom and Dad deserve to know who you really are. We all do."

Carter swallowed around the lump in his throat. "I was afraid you wouldn't want me around Dean anymore," he confessed.

"Please. We're family, and Dean thinks the sun rises and sets on his Uncle Carter. He's been asking about you for weeks." Cat took his hand. "You saw how excited he got when you showed up. I would never tell you not to see him. Being gay doesn't mean you're a pedophile." She shook her head. "I know that. You need to stop worrying about what other people think." She stood up and hugged him tight. "I'm getting cold, and I need to go rescue Mom and Dad. Dean will have them reading to him until midnight if he can get away with it." She released his hand and walked toward the door.

"Thank you," Carter told her softly.

"Nothing to thank me for. We're family—we're supposed to love and support each other." She opened the door and went inside, leaving him alone.

Carter knew he was probably being stupid and letting fear govern him. He'd been through much worse, and as he thought, he realized it wasn't likely his mom and dad would turn their backs on him. Not if Cat had been so supportive. He stood up and walked back into the now quiet house. His mother was in the living room, doing some sort of needlework, and his father sat in his chair, watching television, already half-asleep. "Where's Cat?"

"She left a few minutes ago. Dean is upstairs asleep. He asked to stay overnight," his mother answered without a pause in her fingers.

"I'm going to go to bed as well," Carter told them, then hugged both of them before climbing the stairs. He peeked into Dean's room. He was burrowed under the covers, his blond head sticking out from the blankets, clutching a stuffed rabbit. Carter smiled and then quietly went to his room.

He cleaned up and got ready for bed before slipping beneath the soft, clean, fresh-scented sheets. He'd never thought of his mother as a Donna Reed or Harriet Nelson, but right now, it sure felt like it. He closed his eyes and almost instantly fell asleep, warm and safe at home.

THE FOLLOWING afternoon, after sleeping really late, Carter took Dean to the park. He watched Dean run and climb on the jungle gym, pushed him on the swings, and took him on a nature walk along one of the trails with bridges that crossed a stream. He even helped Dean catch a frog.

"Can I bring it home to Gramma?" Dean asked as he held it inside his hands.

"I don't think Gramma is going to want a frog inside her house. Besides, it lives here. This is his home. He probably has a gramma just like you do," Carter told him. Dean nodded and knelt down on the grass, opening his hand. The small frog hopped away and plopped into the water. "Let's go play for a while," Carter offered, and Dean ran toward the wooden play fort, the frog seemingly forgotten for now.

Carter found a picnic table and sat where he could watch Dean. He seemed to have already found some friends, and they went down the slide, then raced back around to the top.

"He's fearless," a masculine voice said from behind Carter. "Is he yours?"

"My nephew," Carter supplied as the man sat down, also watching the play area.

"Ours is the one in the red," the man said, and Carter turned his attention to a little boy about Dean's age holding a man's hand. "I'm not sure which of them is the bigger kid." The man climbed to the top, guiding the little boy in glasses, and they slid down the slide together.

"Do it again, Daddy," the boy cried, and they ran back to the top. It took Carter a moment to realize the implication of what the child and the man sitting across from him had said. They were a family, the two men and the boy. He seemed to be seeing a lot of gay couples lately, first in New York, and to his surprise, here in Mechanicsburg. Was this a new phenomenon or was he simply seeing them for the first time?

"Dean, ten more minutes," Carter called out. Dean paused and nodded, then turned and ran back to play.

"Do you live in town?" the man across from him asked.

"New York. I'm here to spend some time with my family, and I promised my sister I'd watch him for the day to give her a break. I hadn't planned on it being today, but that's how it worked out."

Dean ran over, and Carter met him and scooped him into his arms, tickling his belly to fits of squirmy giggles. Then he placed Dean back on his feet, and Dean ran back to play. "I'm Carter," he said.

"I'm Cory, and that's Brad with our son Adam," Cory said proudly. Carter watched as the two of them played and then walked over.

"That's it. Papa's just ahead of you," Brad said. Adam raced toward Cory, and Cory scooped him up.

"Are you ready for ice cream?" Cory asked, and Adam threw his hands in the air. "Then let's go." Cory said good-bye, and Carter watched them go. Then he called Dean over and told him it was time to go back to Gramma's.

"Can we stop for ice cream too?" Dean asked, and of course Carter couldn't tell him no. He put Dean in his car seat and drove his mother's car to Bruster's. "What flavor do you want?"

"Chocolate," Dean said excitedly. Carter ordered a kiddie portion for Dean and mint chocolate chip for himself. Once they'd gotten their orders and paid, Carter looked for a spot to sit at one of the outdoor tables, but the place was packed.

"You can join us," he heard a familiar voice say and looked up to see Cory, Brad, and Adam. "There's room."

"Thanks," Carter said and got Dean a seat at the table next to Adam, where Brad was helping him eat his ice cream.

"Adam can only see bold contrast even with his glasses," Cory explained when Carter glanced at them.

"He seems to do very well," Carter observed. Adam largely fed himself, with a little gentle coaching from his daddy.

"He's learning. I'm Brad, by the way." He held out his hand and Carter shook it, introducing himself.

"How old is Adam?" Carter asked.

"Almost three," Cory answered.

"Is there anything they can do for his sight?" Carter asked.

Cory shook his head. "No. Brad and I have been to specialists. I'm a doctor at Carlisle Regional Medical Center, and I've called in all the favors I can think of to get him into the nation's top specialists, but he'll eventually go completely blind." Cory half smiled at Adam. It was obvious that their primary concern was for Adam. "We knew when we adopted him."

"What do you do for a living?" Brad asked.

"I'm a reporter," Carter answered. "For the *New York Press*."

Brad paused. "You wouldn't be Carter Hopkins, would you?" Carter nodded. "I'm a reporter for the *Crier*, and I've been seeing your byline everywhere lately. You snuck in and out of Syria and spent time with the rebels there. Your stories are amazing." Brad turned to Cory. "He broke that story on the mass grave." Brad nearly bounced off his seat.

"Thanks. It was quite a month. I met some amazing people." Carter smiled. "Now I'm working on more in-depth pieces about the life of the fighters and the effect of the conflict on their families. It was a beautiful country. Hopefully, once this is over, it will be again."

"Were you really all alone for a month?" Brad asked, reaching down to wipe Adam's face. "It's all gone," he whispered to Adam and took the bowl and spoon.

"Yes. My editor put me in touch with some contacts from his days as a foreign correspondent, and they made introductions with the group I spent most of my time with. They were an amazing group of men, a real family on and off the battlefield."

"I'd love to be able to do that," Brad said. "But I couldn't leave Adam and Cory for a month."

Carter had the feeling that if he had what Brad seemed to have with Cory and Adam, he wouldn't take those assignments either.

They'd all finished their ice cream, and since there were plenty of people waiting for the table, Carter stood up and said good-bye. Dean said good-bye to Adam, and then they headed for the car. Carter got Dean settled in his car seat and drove home, then parked in the garage and walked toward the house with Dean.

"Mama," Dean squealed and hurried toward her. "Uncle Carter took me to the park. We swinged, and I catched a frog. But he hopped away."

"It looks like you had ice cream," Cat said, pointing to the stains on his shirt. Dean nodded vigorously. Looking at Carter, Cat asked, "So you had a good time?"

"Yeah, I did," Carter told her as they headed inside. Dean was already playing with his toys in the yard, so Carter found a seat, and Cat returned a few minutes later with something to drink and then lowered herself into a chair. She seemed less tired, and her eyes were brighter.

"Me too. I actually got a whole night's sleep and didn't have to get up three times," she said. "Phillip called this morning to say he's coming home tomorrow. He said his current job is over and he'll be home for a while. He's got a few jobs lined up here, and things are picking up, so he shouldn't have to travel so far for work." Phillip was a talented finish carpenter, but with the slump in home building, he'd had to go farther from home to find work. He'd spent the past two weeks working on a high-end resort in New York. They'd agreed to pay him really well, so he'd taken the job, but it had been a burden to Cat. Of course, Carter had found all this out from his mother.

"That's great. He's a great dad, and I know it's hard keeping up with him," Carter said, indicating his nephew, who had worn him out with his constant energy.

"Have you said anything to Mom and Dad?" she asked.

"Not yet. I figure I'll make sure I have a drink or two first to deaden the roar," Carter joked.

"There's nothing to worry about," Cat told him.

"I guess I'm beginning to believe that," Carter said with a sigh. He was really starting to wonder why he'd put off telling his parents for so long. They loved him and worried about him. All he'd done by keeping his secret was isolate himself from them. Carter levered himself up and walked toward the back door.

"Good luck," Cat told him, and he flashed her a quick smile before going inside to find his parents.

CHAPTER FIVE

"OKAY," JOAN said, standing in the living room of his apartment with her hands on her hips. "I don't know what sort of bee flew up your ass, but knock it off."

"What?" Carter snipped.

"Don't give me what and try to sound innocent. You've been moody and... weird for the past three weeks, ever since you got back from your parents. You didn't have a fight with them, did you?"

"No. I told you, they took the news pretty well. Mom still calls the way she always did, and my dad and I talk, so it wasn't anywhere near as big a deal as I thought it would be," Carter confessed.

"Then why are you acting like such a complete shit to everyone? You went out last week and left just after nine. People we've known for years invited you to a party, and you blew it off. No acceptance or rejection—you simply don't respond. That isn't like you, and your mother would have a fit if she knew."

"I don't know," Carter said.

"Do you need to go out and get laid? Because that can be arranged," she told him. "Do something, because moping around the apartment when you aren't at work isn't doing you any good."

"I don't feel much like going out," Carter said.

"Since when? We used to have fun. We didn't go out and get plastered, but you did go out and meet friends."

Carter looked up from where he was sitting. "Do you realize that everyone in our group is with someone except you and me? They all have partners, wives, husbands—except us. Doesn't that depress you?"

"Is that what this is about?" Joan asked. "Because if it is, then I know lots of nice guys. Or is this about you being hung up on a guy you can't have?" Carter groaned softly. "You know I'm right, so just admit it. You're totally hung up on the guy you met in Syria."

"I can't stop thinking about him," Carter finally said, letting the words pass his lips. "I dreamed about him last night, and whenever my mind isn't occupied, it drifts and I end up thinking about him." Carter stood up and wandered into the kitchen, where he pulled out a bottle of wine. He opened it and poured two glasses. He handed one to Joan and then sat back down. "What if we only get one chance to meet that one person in the entire world who completes us, and what if mine was him?" Joan sipped from her glass, listening. "I know it sounds like a ridiculous romantic notion, but it would be just my luck that the guy for me is on the other side of the world, living in a war zone."

Joan set down her glass. "It's not so ridiculous. You're a foreign correspondent. You've been to Iraq, Afghanistan, and now Syria. I happen to believe in fate, and maybe you were destined to find the flower in the field of weeds." Carter shook his head. That analogy had flown over his head. "Think about it. You travel the world spending time in hostile places—if fate has any say, then why *wouldn't* you find your soul mate in a war zone? It guarantees you'll have something in common even if cultural differences seem insurmountable. It also guarantees shared hardship and a joint purpose."

"I don't get it, Joan," Carter said.

Joan picked up her glass, drained it, and set it back on the coffee table. "You've had a good life. Your mom is perfect, and you were raised in a stable home by parents who loved you. There were hardships, I'm sure, but you had an easy life." Joan shrugged. "I'm not saying there's anything wrong with that, but maybe the fates are saying that if you want the love of your life, you're going to have to sweat for it." Joan held out her hand. "Gimme your phone."

Carter unlocked it and handed it to her. After a few seconds, she handed it back, the photo of Nemat displayed on the screen. "Why are you showing me this?" he asked.

"Look at his face and into his eyes," Joan said. "If he was looking at you, then there's little doubt. He's in love with you. He might not have known it, but I would give anything to have a man look at me the way he's looking at you."

"So what are you saying? He's in Syria. The borders are worse now than when I crossed a month ago."

Joan shrugged. "It's up to you. But if you want to find out, you need to figure out a way," she told him. Carter drained his glass and got up to pour another. "It's either that or you can get over him, move on, and let him become part of your past. But you'll always wonder what might have been...."

"Bitch," Carter mumbled as he filled his glass.

"I heard that," Joan said, and he brought the bottle along with him and filled her glass to placate her.

"You do realize I just can't walk across the border, and last time I was there on assignment," Carter said. He knew he was putting up barriers even as his mind raced ahead. Kent would probably jump at the chance to get more exclusive material. The news out of Syria had been bleak for the past few weeks, what little information was getting out at all. "Could this really be possible?"

"It could be if you put your mind to it," Joan told him. "I know your parents will freak out if you go, and I'll worry myself sick, but...."

"Are you kidding? They'll be more freaked about that than the news that I was gay," Carter said, thinking of his mother going through that worry all over again. He hated to put her through it, but the more he thought about it, the more convinced he became that he needed to do this. He *wanted* to do this.

"Jesus," Joan said.

"What?" Carter asked lightly.

"It's like a light just switched on behind your eyes," she told him.

THE FOLLOWING morning, Carter knocked on his editor's open door and sat down in one of the chairs across from his desk. "I want to go back to Syria," he announced and waited for Kent's reaction.

"Today?" Kent asked teasingly. "That's been done. We need something fresh."

"There are other stories I wasn't able to get." He described again the scene outside the mansion. "This is a country filled with stories, and there's no one to tell them."

"Okay," Kent began. "Hold your horses. How do you plan to get in and out? Everyone in that portion of the world is looking for you. Unfortunately in a world as connected as ours, nothing stays secret for long, no matter how hard we try. Hezbollah has put a price on your head. Their entire supply lines from Iran through Syria are threatened because of the impact of your stories. Even some of Syria's friends aren't as willing to help them now. You've single-handedly awakened interest in the conflict here in the US."

"Then that's all the more reason I need to go," Carter countered. "We need to add the icing to the cake. You know in a few more weeks no one will care anymore. That's the way it works. Something else will push the story off the front page. It's our business. But this story is ours. We own it, and if we don't do something to keep our ownership, it will shift to someone else."

Kent paused. "All right, I'll think about it," he promised sternly. Carter knew better than to argue with that tone, so he stood up and left the office. At least Kent hadn't said no. Now Carter needed to truly demonstrate he was serious, and he knew just the thing—he just had to figure out how to make it work.

OVER THE next few weeks, Carter threw himself into his preparations. He was in his apartment, engrossed in his computer, when the buzzer sounded. He jumped at the unexpected sound and then asked who it was. When Joan responded, Carter let her into the building and went back to work.

"You *are* alive," Joan began as soon as she stepped inside.

"I've been busy," Carter said, looking up from his computer screen after answering the question.

"What are you doing?"

"Learning Arabic," Carter answered. "I work on it two hours each night. I won't be fluent, but I figure I'll be able to converse enough that I should be able to pass in a crowd." He looked up at her, and Joan gasped.

"What the hell happened to your face?" She reached out and stroked his skin.

"I got the doctor to give me something to darken my complexion. It'll wear off in a few weeks after I stop taking the pills, but it makes me look more Mediterranean. Before I go back, I'll also dye my hair darker and grow a beard. The way I figure it, if I stand out less, I'll have a better chance of getting in and out without drawing attention."

"What does Kent think?"

"He's impressed. I suspect I'll leave next month for Turkey and cross the border from there," Carter answered, extremely excited.

"Does he know what's got you so fired up to go back?" Joan asked, and Carter shook his head. "Don't you think you should tell him? He needs to know everything."

"I'm going over to work, and I most definitely will. He's instructed me to make contact with the people I worked with to see how things have changed for them." Carter paused. "I don't even know if I will be able to find them. The conflict keeps shifting, and I don't know where they'll be. They could be fighting or at home. Hell, I don't know if Nemat will want to see me. He might have decided I'm better off kept in his past." That was a real possibility. Carter showing up might cause Nemat pain, and he knew he needed to be careful. "So I'm concentrating on my work and getting the best stories I can. The rest is a bonus I keep telling myself I can't count on."

"You're really going to do this?" she asked.

Carter nodded. "You were right. I have to know if what we had was real. I think it was, but like you said, if I don't find out, I'll always wonder." He had gone back and forth for weeks trying to determine how he felt. Should he keep away and let what he felt for Nemat fade into memory? That was the easy way. And he'd been sorely tempted by that. But every time he thought about staying away, he'd come across the picture of Nemat and his heart would lurch. All he had to do was see Nemat's eyes again and his resolve to stay away crumbled. "I know there's a possibility he might not want to see me, and I'll have to deal with that when the time comes."

"There's also the possibility you might not come back," Joan whispered.

"This was your idea, remember?"

Joan sat down next to him. "I know. I'm scared I'm going to lose my best friend. I want you to do what makes you happy. I also want you to be safe and here when I need you. But the two seem to be mutually exclusive."

"They won't be for long. I can't keep doing this forever. I have to think of life after being a war correspondent. So I plan to make this my last trip. If I'm successful, then I will have truly made a difference in the world. If I fail, then…." Carter swallowed at the pained expression on Joan's face. "I know. But…."

"Don't say it, okay?" Joan told him. "And when you tell your mother, don't mention failure to her either."

"I won't," Carter said. "Speaking of which, I need to make arrangements for another trip to see them, and I was wondering if you'd like to come along. Mom asks about you every time I talk to her." He smiled. "She might have given up on making you her daughter-in-law, but that doesn't keep her from asking about you."

"You just want me there to soften the blow when you tell them where you're going," Joan said as she stared at him. Then she sighed and stood up. "Is there any wine?" she asked. She opened the refrigerator and pulled out the bottle of Riesling he had in there. She got two glasses and filled them before carrying them back to the living room. "I'll come with you, but I intend to make myself scarce when you explain to them that you're leaving."

"I don't know yet. Kent hasn't given his final approval."

She took a drink from her glass. "But you think he will."

"I think the prospect of scooping the entire world on a story would be enough for Kent to sell his mother, wife, and children. This is too good for him to pass up, and he knows it." Carter went back to his computer. "I need to get back at this. I have half an hour to go, and then we can go to dinner."

"Where are we going?"

"Middle Eastern, of course," Carter said.

Joan rolled her eyes and drained her glass. "I should have known," she said, getting up. She refilled her glass and sat back down while Carter continued his lesson. When he was done, he put his laptop to sleep, got his coat, and took care of their empty glasses before escorting Joan out of the apartment so they could go to dinner. He reminded himself he had to practice Arabic more when he got back.

A WEEK later, Kent called him into his office to tell him the paper had decided to authorize his trip back to Syria. As before, Carter knew the government and the paper would deny he'd been sent there. His excitement level immediately shot through the roof, as did his level of worry and concern, but there was nothing to do about it now.

"There are some things I want you to tell me before I agree to the expense." Kent motioned toward one of the chairs, and Carter sat down. "I want to know if there's another reason why you want to do this. This assignment will be more dangerous than the last; we know that. But we've seen your dedication to it, quite literally."

"Yes," Carter agreed.

"Almost too much dedication. You've worked and focused on this one thing for weeks. We've seen you change your appearance and learn a new language, and we all commend it, but... we're concerned you want to go for more than just the story." Kent sat down and waited, watching him from across his desk.

"I don't know what to tell you," Carter began.

"How about the truth?" Kent asked. "Did you meet a girl there?"

Carter smiled. "No. I didn't meet a girl there." He reached into his pocket and pulled out his phone. He unlocked it and brought up the photograph. "His name's Nemat. You know him as Amir from the stories."

"Okay," Kent said exaggeratedly. "I don't get it. You want to check that your friend is okay?"

"Yes. But he's… I don't know what he is, except if anyone over there finds out that… he's like me, then they'll kill him."

Kent stared at him for a long time and then his expression changed slightly, the only indication that he understood what Carter was saying.

"I don't care about your personal life," Kent told him. "That's your business. But if your sole reason for wanting this is to be reunited with him, then you need to step back and recheck your priorities. I understand wanting to make sure the people who helped you before are okay. I want that as well, but if this is some crusade to try to rescue or save this man…."

"Kent, I don't know. I know I care for him. I also know there are stories over there that need to be told. His is one of them." Carter thought fast. "Think about it. A few years ago, the president of Iran said there were no gay people in his country. Of course he was full of crap. This man is a freedom fighter. He's no coward—he's a man, and he deserves to have his story told just as much as anyone else. Now, if you don't want me to go, then I'll resign and go on my own." Carter met Kent's steely gaze. "I have to do this, and I will with or without you."

"Dammit," Kent said. "Stories always get screwed up when they mix with personal business."

"They didn't the last time. We got the story of a lifetime. I do my job objectively and carefully, I always have, and passion, whatever the source, comes out in the writing; you know that."

Kent leaned back in his chair. "I can't argue with that. But it still worries me." He sighed. "I won't stand in your way, but you better bring back the story of two lifetimes this time." He motioned toward the door. "Get out of my office and get some work done."

Carter breathed with relief as he stood up and left Kent's office. He'd told Kent the truth. His feelings were so muddled, he wasn't sure how he felt or what he wanted. But he hoped like hell the answer was somewhere in Syria. He sure knew it wasn't here.

He walked back to his desk and went to work. He still had assignments he needed to finish. He worked for hours, completed the stories he was working on, turned them in, and then called his mother. He arranged a visit, and she was thrilled to hear Joan was coming as well. He hung up and finished his final tasks before leaving the office. Once he got home, he called Joan and let her know the arrangements he'd made before booting up his laptop and starting once again on his lessons. The skills he was trying to master were even more urgent now that he was actually going.

After working for hours, listening, repeating, and testing what he'd learned, Carter went to bed. He tried to think of all the things he'd need to do before he left, but all he could think about was Nemat. He could remember every touch, every kiss they'd shared, as though it were yesterday. Each smile and the way Nemat's eyes darkened during passion played in his mind over and over again. He hoped this wasn't just his imagination and that he hadn't imagined the care in Nemat's eyes or the hurt he'd seen when Carter had had to leave.

"It really doesn't matter," he whispered out loud to the quiet room. He had permission, and the paper was going to pay for him to return to Syria. Somehow he'd find Nemat and look into his eyes, and he'd know whether he'd been imagining things. In a few weeks, everything would be made clear. All he needed to do was finish preparing, fly halfway around the world, and somehow sneak across the Turkish border and into a war zone. After that, he had to find Nemat in a country where he had to be careful who he approached. If the reports were right, things had deteriorated in many ways since he'd returned home. "I'm coming, Nemat," he whispered into the darkness, sending the sentiment out into the universe.

CHAPTER SIX

CARTER WALKED down the Jetway at the airport in Istanbul almost a month later. He thought back to the conversation he'd had a week earlier with his mother. To say she'd been shocked at the news was the understatement of the century. Only having Joan in the house kept them from having a complete shouting match. As it was, she'd forbidden him to go.

"Dear, he has to live his own life," his father had told her. She'd alternately glared daggers at him and then at his father before bursting into tears. His father had been unable to console her, and neither could Carter. He'd finally gotten Joan because he'd had no other idea what to do. He knew he should have waited until Cat was there, but she and Phillip were spending some time alone with each other. Somehow, Joan calmed her down, and at dinner his mother was much more herself.

"What did you tell her?" Carter had asked Joan that night when everyone else was in bed.

"I told her the truth. You'd met a man over there and you had to go back to see him. That you had to know if it was real or not." Joan shrugged. "That, she understood."

"So she was upset when I was going over there for work, but okay with it when she thought it was for a man?" Carter asked.

"Oh, she still hates the idea and she always will. You're her son, and she's scared to death that you won't come back. I said she understood. There's most definitely a difference." Joan smiled slightly. "Your mom will be fine. She just doesn't want to see you in danger. She's a mother; it's what they do." Joan had smiled again, and Carter nodded.

"Excuse me," Carter said in Arabic when he bumped into someone on the Jetway. The man mumbled something, and Carter made his way to the baggage-claim area. The signs were in English as well as a number of other languages, but he knew that as soon as he left the airport, some of the language help would vanish.

It took him a while to get through the airport requirements and outside into the September heat. At least it wasn't quite as oppressive as when he'd been here previously. Carter got a taxi to take him to the hotel he'd arranged for the first few days of his trip. He needed to do some research before attempting to cross the border, and he hoped to find people who could help him.

He checked into the hotel, and after he'd spent a few minutes getting settled, he called one of the contacts he'd met the last time he was here. The man agreed to meet him in a café, and Carter made sure he was dressed to blend in as much as possible.

"Carter," Olivier said as he sat down across from him. "I hardly recognized you." He was in his fifties, most likely, with bright eyes, dark hair with a touch of gray, and a chiseled face that must certainly still turn heads. "You look Turkish," he said with a smile.

"Yes. That was the idea. I wanted to be able to blend in."

"You're back for another story?" Olivier asked as he signaled the waiter. He told him what he wanted, and Carter placed his order as well. "So what is it this time?"

"The same as before," Carter told him, and Olivier's eyes widened. "I need to get back into the country."

"You must know that's nearly impossible. Things are getting worse. The fighting goes back and forth. One day the government is in control of an area and the next it's the rebels." He leaned forward. "You know what will happen if you fall into the hands of the Syrian government. And it isn't much better with the rebels." He paused when the server returned with coffee. "No, you should stay away. It's too dangerous."

"I have to go," Carter said with determination. "I've changed my appearance, learned Arabic… I've even brought clothing so I can blend in—something I should have done last time. There are people I have to know are okay, and there are stories the entire world needs to know." Carter sipped from his glass. "Will you help me? There has to be a way in."

"Of course there is. The border is open sometimes and closed others. The government here is becoming alarmed at the number of refugees coming into the country, so they've added patrols. Unfortunately, they overreacted a few times." Olivier sat back and thought while Carter tried his best not to fidget. In order to not appear anxious, he sat back as well and took in the sights and scents of one of the world's great cities. Hagia Sophia rose in the distance, and he stared at the massive dome and minarets that rose toward the sky around it. "I might be able to help you if you're determined to do this."

"I got out the last time by joining a group of refugees. I saw a steady stream of people returning. I could simply join them."

"Not necessarily. There have been reports of people being pressed into service by both sides, and you look like a very able-bodied man. You'd easily gain people's notice. No, I believe you need to cross the border in the country a few miles from the official outpost. The terrain isn't too rough and it's largely deserted." Olivier nodded slowly. "I can get you maps and help with some supplies, but for transportation you'll need to rely on what God gave you." He smiled as their food was brought. "That's all I can tell you. Things have gotten much worse, and the government has become even more paranoid. I have heard reports that they're using chemicals."

"I know. I've heard about them, but in the States they're saying there isn't proof," Carter said skeptically.

"There is, but people in your country don't want to see it," Olivier said. "No one in the world wants to see it, because if they do, then they can't turn a blind eye any longer, and no one wants to get caught up in another Iraq."

Carter couldn't blame them, but he also knew if there was a way for him to find proof of the use of chemical weapons, it would be as big a story as the mass grave and very likely bigger. But he knew better than to say anything. Olivier was baiting him, he was sure of it, and Carter wasn't going to bite. Once he was in the country, he'd sniff out his own story, and if it was chemical weapons, so be it, but he knew there were plenty of others. "I guess I can't blame them," Carter said softly.

Olivier raised his glass and took a sip of coffee. They talked of general topics and a little about Kent. Once the meal was over, Carter paid the bill and thanked Olivier for his help. He arranged to speak to him the following day and then walked back toward his hotel before making a detour into one of the markets. He wanted to get some things to take with him, and while he was at it, he bought some additional clothes for the trip. He wanted to make sure he looked as inconspicuous as possible. That evening he ate dinner at the hotel and then went to bed. He couldn't help thinking of Nemat. He was so close and yet so far. The following day, he met Olivier and got some additional information. He also scouted out the best way to get where he needed to be. It took some arranging, but he bought a ticket on a bus heading to a small town near the border. From there he'd need to make his own way, but he'd done that before. He had an excellent sense of direction and knew he could get where he needed to go. The trick was to do it without attracting attention in a country at war with itself. Once he had his plans set, Carter ate well, packed his things, and made sure everything was ready. He arranged to secure his laptop and other equipment the way he had before and then went to bed. He had what he needed. The fewer people who knew what he planned, the better. The last thing he did before going to bed was make some short calls to his family and to Joan.

Carter caught his bus the following day and dang near sweated through every bit of his clothing during the sauna-like bus ride. No one seemed interested in him, although the driver looked him over as he got on. But other than that, people talked among themselves, the sounds filling the bus as it heaved and rocked across what could barely be considered roads. More than once Carter prayed the old thing would hold together. It seemed to, and eventually they pulled into the small town.

When he got off, Carter gasped for air that didn't reek of sweat and the stench of people who hadn't bathed. He found a small hotel in town and got a room for the night. Luckily, the man behind the desk spoke Arabic and Carter was able to conduct his business with as few words as possible. He paid for the night and then went to his room, which was clean and all he could expect. The bed was hard, and when he lifted the bedding, he found a thin mattress on top of an old door. Not that he cared. He needed to get something to eat, and it wasn't as though he'd be able to sleep anyway. Nemat was across that border a few miles away, and Carter intended to find him.

Carter locked the door as he left his room, making sure anything of value was either on him or hidden as well as possible. Outside, he found a small café that looked like it had been there for hundreds of years. He sat in the evening air and slowly ate. He had food in his pack, but he had little doubt that this was the last cooked meal he'd be getting for a while. As he ate, he listened to the gossip from the other tables, hoping to pick up some bit of information, but he heard nothing he could understand. He finished his meal and paid the bill before returning to his hotel.

He sat awake, looking out his window toward the Syrian border. He hoped against hope that Nemat was all right and that he'd be able to find him. He didn't allow himself to think about what Nemat might feel for him. That was secondary at this point. He needed to know Nemat was all right. Carter pulled one of the small notebooks from his pack and forced his mind onto his work. He had a great nose for a story and knew he could sniff out dozens of them. All he really needed to do was tell the world whatever was going on. He would be the only one with firsthand experience, and he would dang well make the best of it. As Carter watched the shadows lengthen, he hoped he didn't become part of that story. Then he set the notebook aside and closed his eyes, letting Nemat's smile come to the front of his mind.

Hours later, when he decided to give the rickety bed a try, he found he could feel every bit of the underlying door. The mattress masked nothing. He ended up pulling it onto the floor and tried to sleep there with his mind racing and his heart pounding in excitement. Needless to say, sleep eluded him for much of the night. When he did finally fall to sleep, it was only a few hours before his alarm woke him.

In the very first light of dawn, Carter dragged himself out of his makeshift bed, gathered his things, and checked himself in the tiny mirror. He had water, food, and supplies hidden in his pack and on his person.

He opened the door and peered outside. No one was about. Everything around the old building was quiet. Carter stepped out and silently closed the old door behind him. Then he left the hotel, walked through the town, and followed one of the streets until it ended. He stepped off onto the parched ground and took his first steps into what looked like arid grasslands. He knew the GPS coordinates of where he was going. In miles it wasn't far, but he couldn't get an image of wandering alone in the desert out of his mind. He looked back at the town, but he knew this was his only way, so he turned around and put one foot in front of the other.

The first few miles before the sun rose too high were pleasant. The grasses swayed in the breeze, and to his surprise clouds covered the sky. He'd been expecting beating sun, but what he'd gotten was clouds and the one thing he hadn't prepared for: rain. Granted, it didn't last long, but Carter spent much of the time protecting his pack. It was largely waterproof, but he needed to keep it as dry as possible. The rain was warm and lasted less than half an hour. Carter kept going as the sun came out, drying his clothes quickly. A few times he checked his phone to make sure he was still walking in the right direction. He'd veered off course slightly, but was back on track now. At some point he crossed the official border into Syria, but there was no physical indication, just no-man's-land. He should come to the main road near Nemat's family compound soon.

The heat continued building, and he kept walking. He pulled out water and drank the entire bottle. He crested a rise and saw the road just ahead of him. He checked all directions and saw his destination just off to the right. His heart pounded, and he wanted to race over but remained cautious. He needed to check the lay of the land. Before, he'd been an invited guest. This time he was wandering into their home uninvited. He needed to be careful, and prepared to move on. He walked toward the road, which seemed deserted, and slowly approached the compound. It seemed quiet, too quiet, and as he got closer, Carter saw why.

The wall around the exterior was fine, but the main building looked like it had been bombed inside. The walls that remained were blackened and the roof was completely gone, either burned or it had fallen in. Carter approached cautiously, wondering if anyone was here. He didn't call out; it was too eerily quiet for that. He stepped to the gate and peered inside. He didn't see any movement. He slowly walked inside. The plants around the building had been scorched, and what had once been green was now black and shriveled. He moved farther inside and around the hollow shell of the family home toward the back. He remembered other buildings in the compound—maybe they'd survived and that was where the family had taken refuge.

Carter's heart pounded fast and furious. He hadn't realized how much he'd been counting on finding Nemat's family. "Hello," he said softly in Arabic, then listened for a response. He didn't want to yell and call too much attention. A sound reached his ears from behind the house, and he slowly moved in that direction. As he got closer, the sound quieted.

"Who is there?" someone asked in Arabic.

"It's me, Carter," he said after translating it and hoping he got it right. Movement sounded off to his left, and Carter turned as Nemat stepped from out of one of the small buildings.

Carter could barely move and stared at him. "What happened?" he asked, and Nemat's eyes widened.

"A rocket," Nemat answered. "It came a week ago and killed many of my family." He appeared fragile.

"Jalal?" Carter asked.

Nemat shook his head. "He is in the city. He asked me to stay behind to protect the family." Nemat looked around. Then he motioned toward the building he'd come from, and Carter followed him. It was a single room, probably originally built as storage. They seemed to have scavenged what they could save and had moved into here. Carter looked into familiar faces, except now all their eyes were filled with despair.

"Your uncle?" Carter asked, and Nemat nodded. Carter whispered that he was sorry, wishing he knew the proper words to say in Arabic. He nodded to each of the others, and they slowly began to move.

"We saw someone coming," Nemat explained as people left the room. Some continued cleaning up while others worked to make food. "You came back," Nemat whispered once the others had left them alone.

"I had to," Carter told him without stepping any closer. His entire body was drawn to Nemat like a duck to water, but he forcibly kept his distance. "I wondered if you were all right the entire time I was gone." He followed Nemat around the side of what had once been the family home. "Where's Jalal now?"

"Fighting. He's been gone for weeks," Nemat answered and then paused. "You learned my language," he said, flashing a brief smile.

Carter nodded once and then looked around. "Does he know?" Carter asked, pleased all his lessons were paying off.

"No. At least I don't think so," Nemat answered. "He hasn't been back in a long time. The reports out of Aleppo aren't good, and we don't know if he's alive or not. The fighting goes back and forth with no real change, except that the government is becoming more ruthless. They call us terrorists now."

Carter didn't immediately understand him, but he figured out what Nemat had said from context. "They're just words," Carter said. He knew words could be wielded as weapons, but they could also be nothing more than rhetoric.

"They are using chemicals," Nemat said.

"Did the government do this?" Carter whispered.

Nemat shrugged. "We do not know." Carter knew it would be easier to blame the government than other bands of rebels. "It is likely. They have weapons to travel many miles."

Carter wished he knew what he could do to help. "Are there enough food stores for them?" Carter asked. Nemat didn't answer right away, and Carter wondered if he'd expressed himself correctly. Then Nemat nodded slowly.

"We have some, and they will go further now that...." Nemat paused, and Carter watched the sorrow bloom in his eyes. Carter wished he could comfort him but that was impossible, especially publicly. "We will be okay." Nemat turned away for a few seconds, and Carter waited. "What are you doing here?" Nemat whispered when he'd composed himself and turned back to him. "You were supposed to be gone and safe."

Carter looked around. "I spent weeks wondering if you were okay. I convinced the paper to send me back. There are more stories to tell, and I needed to know about you." He couldn't help glancing at the shell of a building that had been Nemat's family home and wondering if it would have been better to stay away. Yes, he was here, but he couldn't do anything to help them. And if he were discovered here, he could bring even more trouble and pain to Nemat's family. "Maybe this wasn't such a good idea," he said softly to himself in English.

Nemat's eyes darkened. "Things are not as you remembered, and I cannot offer hospitality...."

Carter realized what he'd said and how it must have sounded. "No. I didn't mean that. I don't want to cause your family more hardship."

Nemat nodded and turned away. He walked toward the back of the compound, where the women were working to make food. The last time Carter had visited, the food had been wonderful—simple ingredients made to taste amazing. It was obvious that now they were making do with what they had. The women talked amongst themselves, but their voices were filled with worry. Much of what they said went over Carter's head because they were speaking so fast and their voices overlapped, but he didn't have to understand what they were saying to comprehend their fear.

Nemat walked over to where the women were gathered and said something to them. They all turned to look at Carter and then back at Nemat. Their talking recommenced, and Nemat beckoned him over. "They don't believe it's you," Nemat explained.

Carter removed his head covering and smiled at them. One of the women giggled and looked away. She recognized him and then went on to say that he'd gotten more handsome. Carter thanked her and excused himself. As he followed Nemat, a realization washed over him. Nemat was the man of the family, at least until his brother returned. He was responsible for the women and their safety. Nemat had also been responsible for ensuring his relatives who had died had been buried properly, which meant he had most likely dug the graves himself. Carter wished he could offer words of comfort, but he had none. "I don't know what to say except that I feel the loss for your family."

Nemat paused and then bowed his head. "Thank you."

"They were honorable and took a great risk for my safety, as you do now," Carter said.

"This is war. I have seen it, and now they have brought the fight to my family. When I can, I will return and take the fight to them," Nemat said harshly, his eyes blazing, mouth set. "I will cut down their fathers and sons. I will make them grieve as I have grieved." Nemat motioned around him. "They will regret harming my family." He raised his fist above his head and pounded it toward the sky. "I make my vow before all that is holy and good. They will pay for what they've done."

"How?" Carter asked, and Nemat lowered his gaze, still blazing hot. "Are you going to kill yourself to do it?"

"The deaths of my family must not go unpunished," Nemat spat in rapid Arabic that took Carter a few seconds to interpret.

"There are many ways to make people pay," Carter told him, and Nemat paused. "You can't get revenge on the people who did this, because you don't know who they are. But you can make the government pay, and you believe they were behind the attack."

"How?" Nemat demanded.

"My government has said that the use of chemical weapons," Carter said in English, because he didn't know how to express what he wanted in Arabic, "is a line the government must not cross." Nemat nodded. "So if we can prove they did use chemical weapons and make it so no one can turn a blind eye, then they will have to get involved. And if the US joins your side, the government won't stand a chance."

"But they will take over," Nemat said. "Like Iraq."

"That's why they haven't been involved. They don't want to take over. But maybe they will send aid and help. If you get help, that punishes the government, and maybe it will drive Assad from the country."

Nemat didn't look convinced.

"I can't speak for governments and all that. That isn't what I do, but if the Syrian government is using gas, then they're using it on people like you, and that needs to stop." Carter moved a little closer and lowered his voice. "If anything like that happened to you, I'd be after revenge."

"I will help you as best I can, but I cannot go with you. I have to take care of my family."

"I know," Carter said.

"You are welcome to stay here for a few days," Nemat said. "There is some room, and you can share where I have been staying."

Carter wondered where everyone had been sleeping. "Thank you."

Nemat swallowed, and Carter wondered why he appeared nervous. Then he understood. The women were, of course, staying in one area of the compound, and Nemat was staying in another. He wasn't married, and while he was looking after them, there would still be separation between the sexes. Which meant he and Nemat would be alone. Carter swallowed at the implications and tried to push anything carnal from his mind, but his body betrayed his thoughts. If Nemat was nervous and wasn't interested in anything happening, then Carter would keep his distance, even if his imagination was picking up on the possibilities of touching Nemat once again.

Carter wondered what he could do to help, and from what Nemat said when he'd asked, he figured it would be best to stay out of everyone's way. The women made food, and Nemat kept himself busy some of the time, but mostly he sat with Carter and they talked, but largely of nothing.

When it was time to eat, they sat quietly in the single room. The food was simple but tasty, and Carter ate but was careful not to take more than his share. Things had most definitely changed since his last visit, and an additional mouth to feed would burden the family. Carter knew they'd never disregard hospitality, so he was careful to allow enough for the others. By the time the meal was over, night had fallen. Nemat left the room and showed Carter across the compound to a building that had once been used for storage. It seemed solid, and there were cushions on the floor. Care had obviously been taken to make the small room comfortable, and Carter smiled. "We rescued what we could from the house, but there wasn't much we could do. Uncle Nasim was in the room that was hit. He was killed instantly," Nemat told him. "There wasn't much of him left to bury." Nemat's voice broke as he closed the door. "I should not talk about such things."

"Nemat," Carter said softly. "We have saved each other's lives. You can tell me what you wish to say."

"I wouldn't let the women see him," Nemat said. "They were not happy, but there was so little of him left that...." Nemat paused. "I have to be strong. I'm the head of my family, and I have to take care of them and do what's best for them." Nemat stood tall, and some of the doubt disappeared from his expression.

"You buried them, then," Carter said, and Nemat nodded.

"I did it according to our customs. I wish I could have waited until the others returned, but they were buried and the prayers said over them within twenty-four hours, as is required." Nemat spoke almost clinically, like he was afraid of the emotions that would rise. "I was a good nephew and grandson."

"I know," Carter said, lightly touching Nemat's shoulder.

"But I'm not," he said, backing away from the simple touch. "I'm not good."

"Of course you are," Carter said softly.

"No, I'm not. I thought I understood who I was and what I was. But now I'm not so sure. I understand that there are people who believe that what I am...." He lowered his voice. "What *we* are isn't wrong. I've seen it from when I was in Canada; I know there are other opinions. But I can't help thinking that what happened was a punishment from God for my sins." Carter opened his mouth and closed it again. He had no reassurance to give. This battle Nemat was having was his and he needed to work through it and come to his own conclusions. "After the bomb hit and I had buried my uncle, aunt, and grandmother, I sat staring at nothing. My cousin asked me what they'd done to deserve this. She asked me who I thought had sinned to bring this on the family. And I knew it was me." Nemat paced the floor of the tiny room. "I knew I had sinned because I could not get you out of my thoughts. I kept wondering if you had made it and what you were doing. I would do my work in the olive groves and wonder what it would be like to have you with me, working by my side." Nemat stopped and turned toward him. "I knew I was being punished."

"No, you weren't. God doesn't punish people for being who they are. You wishing I was here was no more than what I was doing." Carter stepped closer. There were no windows in the tiny room. It hadn't been built as housing. Thankfully, there were vents near the roof to let the heat escape; otherwise it would be unbearable. "My religious heritage is very different from yours, and there are people where I come from who believe just what you said. All I can tell you is that you're wrong. The God I know doesn't punish people like that. What happened to your home and family had nothing to do with who you dreamed about or what you wanted. It had to do with someone shooting a rocket at your home. Nothing more. We have a saying back home: sometimes shit happens."

Nemat stared at him and then nodded. "I'd say you were right," Nemat said, and then, after a moment of quiet, he added, "I wish I could believe you."

"I wish you could too," Carter said. He placed his pack in the corner. Nemat rolled out the bedding onto the floor and turned out the single, bare light bulb. Carter lay down on the bedding Nemat had indicated and stared up at the ceiling. For weeks he'd wondered what this moment would be like. They were alone together for the first time since he'd left, but even in Carter's sometimes vivid imagination, he never imagined it would be like this. He probably should have, but he'd been hoping for a more emotional reunion.

"Good night, Carter," Nemat said.

Carter said good night as well, but didn't move. The bedding was comfortable enough, but he was wound as tight as a drum. Nemat was so close to him, he could literally reach out and touch him, but he didn't dare. He had no idea if his advance would be welcomed. He was so confused he didn't know what to think. He hadn't expected this to be an easy trip, but he hadn't anticipated this confusion either. "Nemat," Carter whispered into the darkness, but he got no answer. He remained quiet and heard Nemat roll over, followed by a small sigh.

"I thought about you," Nemat said a few minutes later. "I can't lie. I think about you all the time. But I wonder if what we did was wrong. If I was wrong to...."

Carter rolled over and propped his head on his hand. "Did it feel wrong?" Their voices were soft whispers in the pitch blackness. Outside the night was nearly silent, as if everything around them was holding its breath.

"No," Nemat admitted. Carter waited. Whatever happened next had to be Nemat's decision. Carter knew exactly what he wanted. His entire body thrummed with excitement and the need for the man so close to him, but crossing the expanse between them had to be Nemat's decision. It wasn't Carter's decision to make.

He heard Nemat move and held his breath. Then nothing happened. A small shuffling sound was followed by an increase in warmth, and then Nemat was right next to him. Carter reached out and encountered a bearded cheek. He stroked the roughness and then guided their lips together.

Nemat's taste burst on his tongue, and Carter sucked lightly on Nemat's lips. A small moan erupted and was instantly swallowed back. They had to be completely silent. No sound, no whispers. Everything was touch and taste. Carter could more than live with that.

They deepened the kiss. Carter held Nemat close and stilled at a slight sound from outside. Nemat pulled away, and Carter sighed as he heard Nemat quietly moving around him. The sound of metal lightly scraping metal reached his ears, followed by a soft breathing. A floorboard creaked, and then Nemat's warmth was back.

Nemat pressed his lips to him, and Carter silently communicated all the things he wanted to tell Nemat through their lip-to-lip connection. He tightened his hold on Nemat, hugging him close. Carter wasn't sure how far he should take things, but if he only got to hold and kiss Nemat, that would be more than enough. Nemat was alive and whole. That was what Carter really needed to know. He felt Nemat put his hand under Carter's clothes and lightly rub his belly. Carter bit back a gasp as Nemat lightly stroked his skin.

Carter rolled them on the bedding until Nemat lay next to him. Then he backed away slightly and tugged at Nemat's robe. Nemat shifted, and Carter tugged the robe up and over Nemat's head. Carter then pulled off his own clothes, laying them next to him. Then Carter tugged Nemat to him, skin to skin. It seemed so luxurious that he could touch Nemat like this. He slowly explored Nemat's body, using his hands to see what his eyes couldn't at the moment. He memorized the curve of Nemat's butt and the small depression on the side, and the way Nemat's back muscles quivered at his touch. The strength in his shoulders, and the way he shook when Carter stroked up his side. Carter knew he was trying not to laugh and was tempted to stroke there again and again just to hear Nemat's happiness.

Carter slowly rolled them on the bedding again until he rested on top of Nemat. He kissed him hard before stroking the planes of Nemat's chest, warm skin and silky hair passing under his palm. Someday he hoped to be able to see Nemat in all his glory. He knew what Nemat looked like, but only from pieces of information. If he was lucky, someday he'd be able to see every inch of Nemat's brown skin. He dipped his head, tasting Nemat's skin until he found a small nipple. Carter licked and sucked, listening as Nemat stopped another threatened moan.

They were playing with fire, and what they were doing probably wasn't the wisest course of action, but Carter couldn't stop his hands or his lips any more than he could stop instinctual intakes of air. A small gasp broke the silence and was immediately muffled. Carter stroked his hand up Nemat's arm to his hand and found it pressed between his teeth to silence himself. Carter smiled and shifted lower, licking trails down Nemat's amazing skin. He loved the way he tasted: salty, sweet, warm, earthy, like the air around them combined with the spices used in the food. When he reached Nemat's belly, he took extra time, relishing the flutters of Nemat's belly muscles until he came to Nemat's cock, bouncing and pulsing.

Carter stroked him lightly and then wrapped his fingers around the searing hot length before he opened his mouth and sucked him inside. Nemat's cock slid over his tongue, and the flavor Carter tasted on his skin intensified. He sucked him deep and then released him, only to take Nemat deeply once more. Carter felt Nemat tremble beneath him, but other than his breathing, he made no sound. But Nemat's body told Carter everything he needed to know. He was nearly completely rigid, and occasional small gasps for air along with tiny thrusts of his hips told Carter just what he was doing to him. Carter smiled and stroked up Nemat's chest, then lightly tweaked his nipples. He knew the forced silence along with the intense stimulation had to be driving Nemat out of his mind. It certainly was for Carter. He wanted to be able to tell Nemat what he meant to him. But instead he contented himself with showing him.

Carter stilled for a few seconds. Nemat thrust his hips upward. Carter once again took him deep, sucking hard and fast. Nemat's thrusts lost their rhythm, and Carter knew he was close. He continued sucking, running his tongue around the head, teasing him.

He heard a small cry, stifled almost immediately, and then Nemat's flavor burst onto his tongue, intensifying greatly. Carter swallowed what Nemat gave and then slowly drew his lips away.

Nemat sat up on the bedding, breathing heavily through his open mouth, trying to make as little sound as possible. Carter kissed him, and Nemat closed his arms around him and held him tightly. Carter explored Nemat's mouth, letting Nemat taste himself on his tongue.

"Now you," Nemat whispered into his ear and rolled them on the bedding. Carter ended up halfway off on the floor and scooted back on the cushion. Nemat kissed him again and then stroked his skin. Carter arched his back and soaked up the caresses like a cat. Nemat licked and kissed down his chest and belly, mimicking what Carter had done to him earlier.

Nemat ran his lips along Carter's shaft, wetting his skin with heat. Carter gasped and sucked on his own lips to stifle the deep groan that nearly forced its way out. He felt Nemat's tongue on his skin, circling the head of his cock, and then Nemat closed his lips around him. Carter damned near saw stars as Nemat slowly sucked him deeper. Carter touched Nemat's head, stilling him and trying to gently caution him about going too fast. He knew he wouldn't last long. This was what he'd been dreaming of ever since he'd left. He and Nemat were alone, and Nemat wanted him.

Carter swallowed hard and gently thrust forward. He didn't want to overwhelm Nemat, but he needed a little more. He got it when Nemat ran his tongue along the underside of his shaft. Carter gripped the bedding in his fists, his toes curling as he tried to hold off. He didn't last long, and soon pressure built from deep inside. Carter gasped and clamped his eyes closed as his release built and then he fell over the edge, floating on air as he came.

It took him a few seconds before he came back to himself. Nemat rested his head on Carter's shoulder, and Carter held him gently. The cool of the night air worked its way in, and initially Carter was grateful for the relief from the heat, but the cool air soon dried his skin and then began to chill them both. He felt Nemat shiver. Carter kissed him and then Nemat shifted away.

Carter wanted to hold Nemat close all night long, but that wasn't possible. Their momentary interlude was all they dared take. He heard Nemat dressing, and Carter did the same. They would need the warmth tonight. Once he was dressed, Carter climbed into bed and listened to the sounds from outside. There was still very little except the sound of the wind. It was as if nothing else dared to move for fear of drawing a predator. Carter knew the predators were out there.

He felt movement near him, and then Nemat lightly touched his shoulder. Carter took his hand in his, caressing his rough fingers. Then he closed his eyes and burrowed into the bedding. Nemat pulled away his hand, but Carter could still feel his touch as he fell to sleep.

CHAPTER
SEVEN

HE WOKE what felt like almost immediately when he heard excited voices outside. He sat up and looked around. There was light coming in from around the door. Nemat stirred next to him, and within seconds he was out of bed and had the door open. Before Carter could ask him what was going on, he was gone and the door had closed behind him.

Carter listened for a few minutes as the commotion got louder, a mixture of excitement, happiness, and crying reaching his ears. He got out of bed and checked that he looked presentable before pushing open the door and peering outside. Jalal turned to look at him, appearing confused for a second. Then he nodded, and Carter knew he'd recognized him.

He stepped out, and Jalal came over to him and embraced him tightly. "When did you arrive?"

"Yesterday," Carter answered.

Jalal looked around and his momentary joy dissipated. Jalal and Nemat walked toward the burned-out shell of the house, and Carter stayed back, letting the two men share their grief. Carter wanted to ask about the rest of the men he'd met, but now wasn't the time. Jalal needed time to grieve the loss of part of his family, and that was more important. He wasn't sure what to do, so he stayed out of the way and waited for Nemat and Jalal to return.

When they did, they both appeared shaken up. "Nemat says you want to see where the government is using chemicals," Jalal said in his heavily accented English, and Carter nodded. "South of here, in a few villages."

"I have a map," Carter told him, and Jalal paused at his Arabic.

"I will show you, and Nemat will take you there," Jalal said with conviction in Arabic. "Nemat told me what you said to him. You are right. We cannot avenge our family unless we bring pain to the government. You are family. You will be the instrument of our revenge." He reached out and clapped Carter on the shoulder. "Will you do this?"

Carter nodded. "I'll do my best," he said. Jalal looked into his eyes for a few seconds and then turned away. He stood still for a moment and then slowly wandered toward the house. Carter watched as he stepped inside the building.

"This is a terrible shock for him," Nemat said softly. Carter watched as Jalal moved through what was left of the house. "He wants me to help you."

"I don't want to put you in danger," Carter whispered.

"You'll never find what you seek unless I go with you. There are too many patrols," Nemat said. "So I will take you. Jalal knows the way, and he'll tell us what we need to know."

"Why won't he take me?" Carter asked. He was worried about putting Nemat in danger, and if Jalal already knew the way and the lay of the land, maybe it would be better if he went.

"Jalal is the head of the family now. He needs to stay and take care of them. That's his job now. I was only standing in while he was gone." Nemat seemed relieved. "He's also just received the news of what's happened to our uncle. I believe he needs some time...." Nemat added in a whisper, "I'm willing to take you, but if you don't want me with you...."

Carter shook his head. "It isn't that. I don't want anything to happen to you." He lowered his voice. "I came here to make sure you were okay, not pull you into even more danger."

Nemat's eyes burned. "I've seen more death, hate, and sorrow than you have. I'm a man, not a woman or a child that needs to be protected. I'm able to take care of myself, and you, if necessary." Carter didn't know why, but he'd often thought of Nemat as an innocent, and he saw now he'd been wrong. Nemat had seen things Carter couldn't imagine. He'd single-handedly buried his family members and looked after the remaining people. He was strong, resourceful, and intelligent. As Carter thought about it, he realized Nemat would make a wonderful guide and companion. Jalal looked like a soldier, but Nemat looked much more innocent, something that could very well come in handy.

"Yes, you can, and I'm sorry. I would very much like you to come with me." Carter smiled nervously. Traveling any distance in a country torn apart by civil war wouldn't be an easy task. "Did Jalal have any idea how we should travel?"

"We'll need to go over land and stay away from the roads. He needs some time to himself, and after the midday meal, we will talk and plan," Nemat told him. Carter nodded and tried to keep his patience under control. Nemat had work to do, and Jalal needed time to deal with his loss. Carter went inside the room he'd slept in and got his pack. He made sure his things were set. There was power, so he got his adapters and made sure everything was charged. He also made notes on what he wanted to do and took the time to get his thoughts together. Then he found Nemat and spent the rest of the morning helping with whatever tasks he could.

THEY ATE a very subdued lunch, and then he, Nemat, and Jalal gathered in the small room where Carter and Nemat had slept. This time when the men gathered, there was no pipe smoking and no lighthearted conversation.

"The villages where the government is rumored to have used gas are south of here, near the mountains," Jalal said. Carter pulled out his map, and Jalal showed him. "There are few major direct roads between here and there. It's mostly grassland and desert. But there are smaller ones, and those are the ones you must take." He pointed to the route. "I used to go there when I was a boy. Our father loved the mountains and used to take us there on trips." Jalal paused and appeared nostalgic for a few seconds. "We can't spare the truck, but you can take the car." Carter nodded as he followed the conversation. Sometimes it took him a few seconds to interpret what was being said, but he thought he was doing pretty well. "It's old but it should get you there."

"What if something happens to it?" Carter asked. It was a distinct possibility that whatever vehicle they started out with wouldn't return.

"Get your story, help my people, and make sure my family didn't die in vain, and it will be worth the loss of the car," Jalal said sternly. "Everyone is worried the government is becoming more desperate and that they'll begin using chemicals on everyone. If this is the way to stop them, then we will help." Jalal's eyes blazed with fury, and Carter held his breath for a second, wondering if the anger and frustration pent up inside Jalal would erupt. There was only so much any man could take, and Carter could see that Jalal was nearing his breaking point.

"I appreciate it, and I will do everything I can to try to do that," Carter said. *To hell with objectivity.* If he were home, he'd have been pulled from the story because he was getting too close, but here, he was the only option. He needed to gather his evidence, get his story, and get out of the country. He reached out and took Jalal's wrist. "We will do everything we can."

Jalal gripped Carter's wrist in return. "We will gather what supplies and water as we can spare. It won't be a lot, but too much would attract attention." Jalal paused briefly. "There will be patrols, I can almost guarantee it. Say you're trying to visit family in Tadmur. Uncle Habib has died, and you are traveling to the funeral. It's that afternoon and you only have a few hours. Even government soldiers will understand that—they have families as well." Jalal paused again. "The only issue is that Nemat looks army age. They will wonder why you aren't in the military. The freedom fighters will be no problem, but government units will ask."

Nemat leaned forward and began to cough. After a few seconds, Carter swore he was going to cough up a lung. Then he sat back up and smiled. "How's that?"

Jalal shook his head. "Perfect. They'll think you're dying and will probably back away in case they could get sick as well." He turned to Carter. "Speak as little as possible. Your Arabic isn't bad, but you sound Saudi. Let Nemat speak, if at all possible, and keep your eyes down. You're both on your way to a funeral, so looking serious and sad is good."

They both nodded, and Carter turned to Nemat, his heart racing. This was what he lived for, to get into areas and root for stories no one else was willing to try to find. He also knew this excursion would be very dangerous, especially as they got closer to the villages.

"We'll keep our wits about us," Nemat said.

"I know you will," Jalal said. "You have proven yourselves in battle, and you'll do well here too." Carter reviewed the route they were going to take one more time. He memorized it and then folded up the map before placing it in his pack. They would need it again, and thankfully the legend was in Arabic, with no indication that he could see that it was foreign. "Both of you get some rest today."

Carter nodded and stood up, then left the building. Just before closing the door, he saw Nemat and Jalal laying out prayer rugs, and left them alone. He wandered back away from the house and into the grove of olive trees. He sat in the shade of one of the gnarled trees and said his own silent prayer. He'd pretty much given up religion once he moved to New York and realized he was gay. The fire and brimstone he'd been brought up with didn't have meaning for him any longer. The funny thing was, he didn't pray for himself or his own safety, but for Nemat.

After a while Carter looked up and saw Nemat walking toward him. Peaceful happiness washed over him. It only lasted a few seconds as a low-pitched rumble, like thunder, sounded in the distance, reminding him where he was, the danger that surrounded both of them.

Nemat sat down next to him. Neither of them spoke or moved. Carter wished he could do something as simple as touch Nemat's hand, but he didn't dare. "In some cities," Carter whispered just above the sound of the wind through the leaves above, "we would be able to hold hands and even dance together."

Nemat nodded. "I saw places like that when I was in Canada. My father was appalled, but I was fascinated. My friend Mark explained them to me."

"What about Jalal?" Carter asked, watching Nemat's older brother.

"I don't know. It wasn't something we spoke about other than a few words from father as we hurried past one of those places," Nemat said. "Of course, I kept my interest to myself. I must have been fourteen, but I knew there was something different inside me." Nemat shifted so he had a better view of the compound. "I hoped it would go away, but it never did. I wished and prayed for hours. But as I got older, the feelings intensified." Nemat shifted his gaze to the ground.

"What happened?" Carter asked.

"There was another boy in school, and he kept looking at me when he didn't think anyone could see. After a while, I started to look back. But I was shy and quiet, while he was loud. I wondered if he was like me, because when he'd look at me... things would happen." Color bloomed on Nemat's cheeks. "One day we were playing outside and some of the other boys began calling him names. I didn't know what they meant, but I knew it was bad. After that I stayed away from him. We'd just gotten back from Canada, and I was suspect anyway because of where we'd lived." Nemat sighed. "One day he wasn't in school. The instructor had said that he'd been"—Nemat paused for a second—"enrolled at another school, but the kids had another explanation. His parents had found out about his feelings and they sent him to a place where they could fix him."

"Oh, God," Carter said softly.

"When I saw him again, there was nothing left of the boy who used to laugh and play. His eyes were hollow, and he was very quiet, like the life had been driven out of him."

"What happened to him?" Carter asked.

Nemat shrugged. "He stayed around for a while, and when he was old enough, he... left. I heard he was in Beirut. They're more... open there. I hope he's happy now."

"Are you?" Carter asked. Nemat turned to him, but didn't answer the question right away.

"My family is here, and I need to help take care of them. It doesn't matter if I'm happy. They need me." Nemat had evaded the question, but Carter understood just as clearly as if he'd answered. He wanted to argue with him. It was important if Nemat was happy because it mattered to him. But explaining what was possible in the outside world would only bring Nemat pain and longing for things he couldn't have. "Does your family know?"

"Yes. I told them when I got back," Carter said.

"They didn't send you away?" Nemat asked.

"No," Carter said. "I was afraid of how they'd react, but they are trying to understand. I was raised very conservatively. Different religion, but much the same message as the one you received. So, like you, I kept quiet about who I was to most people around me. I dated girls when I was in high school, and even had a scare that I might have gotten a girl pregnant." Carter rolled his eyes when he thought about how stupid he'd been and how close he'd come to ruining his life, and hers, over that decision. "After that I was more careful."

"Why did you tell your parents?" Nemat asked.

"After I got home the last time, I realized how short life can be. I saw what was happening here and how wonderful your family was in the midst of everything, and I came to the conclusion that life is simply too short. So I took the train to visit them and had a talk with my mom and dad. They were angry at first."

Nemat nodded.

"Not for the reason you think. They were angry because while they didn't understand, they still felt I should have told them. They were hurt that I kept it from them." Carter paused. "They equated my silence with lying to them, and it wasn't the same. I wasn't ready to accept who I was, and until I did that, I hadn't been able to tell them."

"I could never tell my family," Nemat said. "The only reason I'm not being pressured to marry is because of the war." Jalal came out back, saw them, and started walking in their direction. He spoke rapidly to Nemat. Unfortunately, Carter only caught part of it. Nemat answered that whatever Jalal was searching for was gone.

Jalal nodded and turned away before walking back toward the house.

"You can sit with us," Carter said.

Jalal stopped and turned, but then shook his head before heading back.

"He needs time alone," Nemat whispered. "Jalal is very strong, but he feels deeply, with passion. Uncle Nasim was very close to Jalal. They spent a lot of time together. He was good to me too, but he and Jalal had a special… bond?" Nemat said, changing to English. "Jalal needs to appear strong, so he will grieve openly only when he's alone. After our parents died, I cried with the others, but Jalal never did. He remained strong. Everyone thought he was made of stone, but I heard him at night when everyone else was asleep."

"I never would have guessed," Carter said. He pulled his legs to his chest. "When the war's over, will you travel?"

"Away from here? I hope to. I want to be able to see the world. Jalal would stay here and be happy for the rest of his life, but I want to go where I can be… free." Nemat stared. "From here I can almost pretend everything is okay. The house looks normal, and I can imagine my aunt and uncle walking out to find me." Nemat looked through the grove of trees.

Carter followed his gaze. "Did your parents live here too?"

"No. They had a big house in Damascus. At least, it seemed big when I was small. After they died, we left and came here. Uncle said the house was sold, and after that he planted this grove of trees. I always think of my parents when I come out here. During the dry months, we sometimes have to pump water from the spring for them, but they make fruit every year and give us plenty to eat. Uncle said once that there was money in a bank somewhere for Jalal and me, but we never heard anything more about it. And by now it's probably gone."

"It depends where your father deposited it," Carter said. "If it was in Canada, then it could still be there."

Nemat didn't seem interested, and Carter didn't pursue it. Nemat stood up and extended his hand, then pulled Carter to his feet. "I can show you the spring, if you like."

Carter followed him through the grove to a green area off to the side of the property. "Wow," Carter said as they approached. "It's beautiful. Why didn't your uncle build the house here?"

"It's too wet, and it would be bad luck. The desert would take offense and the spring could dry up," Nemat explained. Carter nodded. Disturbing the land could interrupt the flow of water and the spring would move elsewhere. Green plants hugged the spot where the water sprang from the ground. A small stream ran over rocks and sand. A gasoline-powered pump sat near one end of a deep pool. "This is where we pump water for the trees and the house. But now we don't have enough gas, so the women bring water for us to use."

"Are we going to be using the gas that could be used to pump water for the family?" Carter asked.

"Yes... and no. I pump only for large needs. Right now is the rainy season, so we get water ourselves. When it gets dry, I pump water to fill the tanks."

Carter wandered through the green area. The ground was sandy but covered with vegetation. Carter followed the small stream as it wound around rocks, growing smaller and smaller until it ended in a bed of wet sand, disappearing back into the desert. "Do you have animals?"

"We used to. Not anymore," Nemat said sadly. "We had goats but... the war. They were taken to feed the fighting men. Now we'll wait for the war to be over and maybe get more."

Carter slowly turned around. This was a beautiful spot, and without the war, would be ideal—water, trees, animals, olives, everything needed for life, all right here. "Did you ever go swimming?"

"We used to play in the water, but that was all," Nemat answered.

Carter bent down and scooped some of the water in his hand. "It's cold," he said. He'd expected it to be warmer. He should have realized. The water came from aquifers deep in the earth. It was the sun that would warm the water, and there wasn't time.

"We used to go in on the hottest days. But we weren't allowed at other times. It's the water source for everything here, so it needed to remain as pure as possible." Nemat smiled. "We used to have water fights, though. We'd sneak buckets out of the sheds and come down here when the sun was high. We'd throw water on each other. We'd be cold for a few seconds, and then the sun would warm us back up." Nemat bent down, swirling his hand in the moving water. "It was a good place to grow up." He crouched and watched the water. Carter remained quiet so he wouldn't disturb Nemat's thoughts. "It *was* a good place to grow up, but not any longer."

"It will be again," Carter said, but Nemat shook his head.

"I don't think so. What's good about this place is being destroyed piece by piece. No one seems to want the same things, and all we do is kill each other," Nemat whispered. "I used to wonder how people could leave, but I don't anymore." He stood up, but continued looking toward the water, his back to Carter. "There's little hope here for me."

Carter opened his mouth to say something, and Nemat turned around. "We should go back," Nemat said, looking at the sky. "There are still preparations we need to make, and once it gets dark, it will be impossible. The light will make us a target." He led Carter back to the compound, to a small building near the edge of the olive grove. Nemat swung the doors open and walked inside.

An old car sat on the dirt floor. It looked like it was on its last legs, but Carter already knew appearances could be deceiving. "Who keeps the car and truck running?"

"Me," Nemat said with a smile. "I love working on cars, but this one is coming to the end. Parts are hard to find. It runs good now, but maybe not for too much longer." Nemat shrugged, opened the car door, and turned the key in the ignition. The engine rumbled to life, and Carter stepped back. It sounded like hell, and he half expected the old thing to explode at any second. "Don't let the noise fool you," Nemat called over the racket. "It's supposed to sound that way." Nemat turned off the engine, and Carter shook his head to clear out his ears. "I had to make it noisy or others would try to steal it."

"Are you serious?" Carter asked. "It sounds close to death."

"It is fine," Nemat said, patting the old battered hood of the once blue sedan. The desert had worn away much of the paint, so now it was blue and primer gray, with bits of rust here and there. Nemat motioned Carter around and started the engine once again. Then he pointed to the fuel gauge. Carter's eyes widened.

"How will we get there with no gas?" Carter asked. The needle hovered at a quarter tank.

"It's nearly full. I changed it so people would think it was near empty. They will not steal a car out of gas," Nemat said with a sly grin. "When it gets empty, it goes lower, but never higher."

"You're sneaky," Carter said. Nemat smiled and went to lift the hood. He looked beneath and seemed to be checking things over. Carter knew nothing about cars, so he stepped back and watched, trying not to appear to be staring at Nemat's backside. Eventually Nemat closed the hood with a bang. "We are ready to go," he pronounced.

Carter nodded and moved back. Nemat closed the doors, and they walked into the compound. The women were making dinner. Carter looked around for Jalal, but didn't see him. Nemat didn't seem surprised and busied himself while Carter got his things together and went through his pack for the second time that day. He was getting nervous and wanted to make sure he had everything.

Food was ready an hour later, and everyone gathered to eat. Once again, it was subdued, with the women remaining largely separate from the men. Carter knew it was because he was an unmarried male who wasn't family. He finished eating and thanked both Jalal and Nemat, then nodded to the women before making his excuses. He was more nervous now than he'd been sneaking into the country. Here, he wasn't too far from the border, but they would be traveling deeper into the heart of the country.

He sat outside, watching the sky as the light faded and the stars made their appearance. "I used to stare at the stars all the time when I was young," Carter said when Nemat came over and sat next to him.

"Me too," Nemat said.

"You know, growing up, we were on opposite sides of the world, but each night, we saw the same stars. I stared up at the same ones you did." At least the stars were largely the same ones. He'd been farther north, but some of the constellations were the same. They were simply in a different position in the sky. Carter looked for familiar patterns and found the dragon and Perseus. The ones most familiar to him weren't visible, but it didn't matter. There were new patterns, and he spent some time trying to remember them.

"My mother used to believe that the future was written in the stars," Nemat said.

"Astrology," Carter said, and Nemat hummed. He said what they called it, but Carter was fairly sure it was two names for the same thing. "My mother used to read her horoscope every day." She hadn't believed in it and often thought it silly, but she still read them. It was one of the things Carter had always found strange about his religious mother. "I bet our mothers would have liked each other."

Nemat hummed again, and they became quiet, the cooling night air adding a chill. After a while, Nemat stood up, and Carter did the same. He followed him to the small room where they'd slept. He expected to see Jalal, but the room was empty. They made up the beds like they had the night before, leaving room for Jalal, and then lay down and turned off the light. Nemat whispered a soft good night and Carter did the same, but tonight there was no hand-holding, and Nemat definitely didn't move closer to him. Carter stared into the darkness, aware every time Nemat shifted on his bed.

At some point, Jalal came in the room. Carter heard him shifting for a few minutes, and then all was quiet. Carter closed his eyes and tried to sleep, but his mind had other ideas. He kept replaying the night and day he'd had with Nemat. He'd had a chance to truly get to know him. Carter knew those quiet memories would likely be all they would be able to make for a while, maybe ever.

CHAPTER EIGHT

CARTER HELD on to the dash as they drove. Now that they were moving, he knew it wasn't the engine of the old car he needed to worry about, but the suspension. He was being shaken apart. Initially, the road had been fine, but they needed to go cross-country to avoid patrols, and as soon as Nemat turned onto a narrower road, Carter wondered how in the hell they were going to make it.

"We are fine," Nemat told him, but Carter held on for dear life as the steering wheel wrenched in his direction and then back toward Nemat. He kept expecting patrols or groups of soldiers to appear at any moment, but so far they'd largely been alone.

Ten minutes later, Carter's fears were realized when he saw a group of men clustered by the side of the road. Nemat turned to look at him, and Carter swallowed hard. Then Nemat turned forward once more. A man in camouflage stepped out in front of them, machine gun at the ready. They were well equipped and obviously from the army. Nemat slowed to a stop, and the man held his gun tighter. Another soldier approached Nemat, who lifted his hands away from the steering wheel. He said something to Nemat, who answered. Carter did his best to keep up with the conversation, but they were speaking so quickly, and he had to translate everything in his mind, so he quickly lost track of what was being said. He knew Nemat had explained about going to the funeral and saw the men look at him more than once. Jalal had told him to remain as quiet as possible, and it seemed to be working.

Then the soldier called to him, and Carter lifted his gaze, keeping his face angled so the man didn't get too close a look. His heart pounded, and he expected the soldier to turn to the man in front of them at any second and give him the order to open fire. The soldier barked something, and Carter glanced at Nemat, who turned to the soldier and rolled his eyes. Nemat said something. They must have slipped into a local dialect, because Carter couldn't understand a word. The man in front of them moved closer, and Carter's leg began to shake. He expected the car to be riddled with bullets within seconds, and then both he and Nemat would be dead. His mouth went dry, and he glanced at Nemat and then at the soldier. Nemat slowly reached to a small compartment in the dash and pulled out some papers. He handed them to the soldier, who looked at them and then turned to the other men, who were all coming closer to the car. They were sunk, Carter just knew it. The soldier looked over the papers and then handed them back to Nemat. He said something, and Nemat laughed along with him. The man in front of the car walked to the side of the road, and Nemat slowly began to pull forward.

Carter hardly breathed until they'd left the checkpoint behind them. "I couldn't understand a thing they said."

"They were speaking like locals," Nemat said. "It was their way of testing that I was telling the truth."

"What did you tell them that was so funny?" Carter asked, not sure he really wanted to know.

"I said you couldn't speak. I was hoping you'd stay quiet."

"What were those papers?"

"Identity documents. I said yours were lost when the rebels bombed your house."

"Is that why you sounded angry?" Carter asked as the bone-shaking bumps continued.

"Yes. No one really knows who's on what side any longer, so everyone is suspicious of everything and everyone."

"I'm surprised they didn't want to look in the trunk," Carter said.

"That's not why they're there. They are hoping to stop large-scale movement of fighters from reaching Aleppo. They really aren't interested in two men in a car, heading away. Returning will be a whole different matter," Nemat said. They drove for a while longer and then turned onto an even smaller road. They appeared to be heading back the same direction they'd come. Then after a while, they turned again.

"Are we getting close?" Carter asked, holding on once more.

"We should be," Nemat answered. Carter watched for any signs of life, but saw nothing but open land. Eventually what looked like a small settlement appeared on the horizon. Nemat headed for it, and Carter kept his eyes glued to the buildings. He expected to see people, but the place appeared deserted.

"Where is everyone?"

Nemat slowed and glanced at him, the expression in his eyes telling Carter what he needed to know. This was most likely a ghost town. Nemat stopped the car, and they sat for a few seconds, looking over what had once been homes, now quiet.

"This has to be the right place," Carter whispered as a chill went up his spine. He got out of the car and waited for Nemat. The only sound that reached his ears was the wind. Everything else was silent. No people talking, no children playing or dogs barking, goats bleating… nothing at all.

He followed Nemat up into the village, watching where he placed his feet for each step.

"It feels like walking on the dead," Nemat whispered. Carter couldn't have agreed more.

They made their way through the buildings, looked inside each one and then moved on. Carter half expected to find bodies, but there were none, at least not that they found, just emptiness. "It looks like everyone left," Carter said.

"They did not leave," Nemat said and pointed inside a small house. The smell that wafted out made Carter's eyes water and his stomach turn. He peered inside and saw a dead dog lying on the floor. "It was the chemicals. The wind has blown them away."

"I know," Carter agreed. "But you could almost believe everyone simply left."

"How do we prove it was chemicals?" Nemat asked.

"We need to find the casings," Carter said. "If chemical weapons were used, they were delivered in shells that dispersed the chemicals when they exploded. Those shells will have small traces of any of the chemicals used on them. If we can find any, then we can take a sample, and I can have them tested when I get out of the country." He thought about trying to take a sample from the dead animal, but there was no way he was going anywhere near that thing. It was too nasty. "Are any of the buildings damaged?"

Nemat paused. "Why?" he asked and then pointed at a small house across the square.

"Chemical weapons don't cause damage, but the delivery shells can," Carter explained as he went where Nemat had pointed. "Let's try there." Carter figured whoever killed everyone here must have ultimately buried all the people as a cover-up. The military would probably have policed any of the shells or remaining ordnance, but they might get lucky.

They walked to the small house. The place still smelled of burned wood and what might have been cooked flesh. He wasn't sure, but hesitated before peering inside. The fire had burned everything, leaving little for them to look over. Nemat stepped inside and carefully picked his way through the remnants of someone's life. Carter followed, but saw nothing that would help.

"Where did the shells come from?" Nemat asked as they stepped back outside.

Carter took a deep breath of fresh air to clear his lungs and settle his roiling stomach. He looked around and saw what appeared to be another burned home. It didn't look like the fires had spread, so he followed lines from the homes to a vantage point overlooking the town. "I bet they were up there," Carter said. He then made a visual line back. "Let's try back here."

Nemat nodded and led the way. Carter wanted to ask him to go back to the car. There was danger here. Carter could feel it in his bones, and he didn't want Nemat hurt. But he didn't want to injure his pride either. "You don't have to do this," Carter said.

Nemat stopped. "You think I'm scared?" he challenged.

"No. I'm scared. I don't want you to get hurt," Carter admitted, hoping Nemat understood where his concern originated. "I'm doing this because I agreed to find out what was happening. This is my job," he whispered.

"And I'm here because I don't want anything to happen to you," Nemat told him firmly. Carter widened his eyes in surprise as Nemat crossed his arms over his chest, daring Carter with his expression to contradict him.

Carter had no idea what to say and simply stared at the beautiful man in front of him. Nemat had just given him as close to a declaration of love as Carter figured he was ever going to get. "Then let's go," he said, swallowing hard.

If they were anyplace else, Carter would have pulled Nemat to him and kissed him for all he was worth, but neither of them could chance that. Not here. If they were caught here at all, it would be bad enough for them, but being caught like that would mean an instant death sentence. Carter motioned around the back of the burned-out buildings, where they found a narrow street. He looked down each passage between the mud-and-brick dwellings, inside each house, and checked in the yards.

"Over here," Nemat whispered, and Carter hurried over. Nemat pointed to the remnants of a shell casing. Carter made his way between the buildings and stopped. He opened his pack, pulled out a plastic bag, and turned it inside out. He carefully used the bag as a glove and captured the first piece of metal, making sure not to pierce the piece of plastic. Then he sealed the bag and got a second. He picked up the rest of the pieces and got them in bags. Then he pulled out his phone and kicked himself for not taking the pictures of the pieces before he touched them, but he took pictures of where they'd been. Then he took pictures of the surrounding area to prove where they were, as well as a GPS reading.

Carter put his phone away and retrieved his notebook, then wrote the facts and jotted down ideas to help trigger the story he wanted to write.

"You seem so different," Nemat said, and Carter paused. "For a few seconds it was like I wasn't here."

"When I'm working, I sometimes get caught up," he explained as he finished writing his notes. Then he placed the bags and his notes in his pack. He wasn't thrilled with carrying them on him, but had no choice. After hoisting it onto his shoulder, he looked around again. "Let's make one more pass to see if there's anything else for us to see. Then we need to get out of here." This place was giving him the creeps.

Nemat agreed and they began making their way through the empty town. They'd probably gotten halfway through the town when a whistle sounded overhead. Carter barely had a chance to react before he found himself pushed to the ground as an explosion erupted from the other side of the village. The ground shook, and Carter covered his head.

"We need to go!" Nemat said. He scrambled to his feet and pulled Carter along behind him. They took about ten steps before another explosion sounded, this one closer.

They ran, weaving between buildings, trying to get back to the car. Explosions continually sounded from behind them, the air filling with dust. They kept running and reached the far side of the village. Nemat pulled open the driver's door on the car and dove inside. Carter got around to the passenger side and jumped in. Nemat already had the engine running and jammed the car into gear before Carter had a chance to fully close his door.

"Get down," Nemat ordered, and the car jumped forward.

Carter expected them to be blown off the road at any minute, but the explosions continued behind them, slowly becoming more and more distant. A loud boom rocked the car, the rear end fishtailing for a few seconds, then the tires caught and the car jumped forward.

"Jesus, that was close," Carter muttered, hoping like hell they'd put enough distance between them and the shelling, although that would likely be only a temporary reprieve. Carter's heart raced, and he stared at Nemat, surprised at how calm and focused he was. There was no sign of concern or the panic Carter felt welling up inside him, only determination.

They moved faster and faster, the car lurching and bouncing, throwing Carter around. He bit his lip, closed his eyes, and prayed like hell that they got out of this alive. The seconds ticked by, becoming minutes. They had to be putting some distance between them and whoever was shelling the empty town.

"What was happening?" Nemat asked. "Why would they bomb an empty town?"

"Don't know," Carter answered. "Maybe the government is trying to get rid of the evidence." They continued moving, and Carter allowed himself to relax a little. He lifted his head and peered behind them. No one seemed to be following, which struck Carter as some sort of miracle. Maybe the troops didn't view them as a threat and had only wanted to scare them away. If that was their goal, it had most certainly worked. Carter had no real idea and was simply grateful to be away from there and still in one piece.

Nemat sped up even more, and Carter thought his insides were going to be shaken out. They rode for what had to be ten or fifteen minutes before figuring they were in the clear. If someone were coming after them, it would have happened by now. Carter took a deep breath and released it as a bang sounded from beneath the car. At first he thought they'd been shot, but the car simply coasted to a stop and everything became quiet. Rumbles that sounded like thunder echoed in the distance.

"We need to get out of here," Carter said, pushing open his door. He grabbed his pack, and Nemat got a bag from the backseat. They hurried away from the car. "What do we do now?" Carter asked.

"We walk," Nemat told him. "We aren't far from the main road. We shouldn't use it directly, but we can walk close to it and use it to guide us home. Normally, people will offer rides."

Carter shook his head. Catching a ride from the wrong person could leave them both in a world of hurt. The rumbles continued from behind them, traveling through both the air and ground. "We might as well start. We have enough food and water for a while." Carter turned around. "I'm sorry about the car."

Nemat shrugged and lifted the cooler of provisions he'd brought. Then they began walking.

There were a number of things Carter found out in a very short time. Each footstep raised a mini cloud of dust that got everywhere.

It mixed with his sweat, and he ended up a muddy, crusty mess. He could deal with that, but it didn't take long before the sand chapped his skin. He also determined that thinking about the fact that they were walking through a desert made him thirstier by the second. It didn't matter that he didn't usually drink constantly—he suddenly needed to now. He was grateful for the light clothing that let his skin breathe while covering him from the constant sun. "We need to make the water last," Nemat scolded him after Carter reached for yet another bottle.

"Sorry," Carter said.

"We'll stop to eat once we reach some shade." Nemat pointed to a few trees that broke the horizon in the distance. "Until then, we need to keep moving in order to put as much distance between us and the troops as we can."

Carter was all in favor of that. The more he thought about it, the more Carter realized he was most likely right: the government was destroying the village to wipe out any evidence and would then try to blame the destruction on the rebels to further muddy the waters. Keeping the story muddled would buy them time, and the current regime was all about delay. The murkier the situation became, the better the government's position was. "Good idea," Carter said, pulling his thoughts back to their current situation. "How far are we from your home?"

"If we don't run into patrols, twenty, thirty miles. If we do, then we add distance to stay away," Nemat told him as though it were a normal thing to walk that far in the sun and heat. "At least we are going in the right direction."

Carter had no argument for that, and there was no other solution. They needed to keep moving regardless of what they encountered or how uncomfortable he might be.

They trudged on, talking very little. Carter remembered he had his sunglasses in his pack, and he put them on. At least they provided some relief from the sun. After what seemed like a very long time, they reached a small group of scrubby trees. They sat down in the little shade the trees provided and devoured the food that had been packed for the trip, leaving some for later. Carter knew they were going to need it. Walking again was murder. Once he'd stopped to rest, he didn't want to start again, but he forced his legs to work. Carter's muscles ached and his skin burned as they continued walking. Sweat welled on his skin and then evaporated, keeping him dry and making him thirstier. He tried not to think about it, but water was ever present in his mind. Eventually, they ate the rest of the food and further limited their intake of water. As the sun moved lower in the sky, Carter became happier the more his shadow lengthened and when the grassland was bathed in the red of a spectacular sunset. Not that he took more than two seconds to notice it. He was already aware that the temperature was dropping, and with no light, they would need to find a place to stop.

"There's a creek bed over there," Nemat said, pointing, and Carter followed him, picking up his pace, pushing his fatigue away at the thought of water. When he crested the small culvert, he looked down inside, expecting to see water. Nemat had neglected to tell him it was a *dry* creek bed. He huffed and turned to Nemat, ready to erupt.

"We'll need shelter," Nemat said, and Carter pursed his lips, holding back his frustration. None of this was Nemat's fault, and he needed to remember that. The fault was his. He was the one who needed to get the story, and Nemat had taken him. If he had to be angry with anyone, it should be himself.

"Okay. Do we start a fire?" Carter asked.

Nemat looked around and gently shook his head. Of course, other than the grass, there was nothing to burn. They didn't need to draw attention to themselves anyway. So there was nothing for them to do except last out the night.

They found a place where the ground was firm and not too rocky. They sat down and Carter opened his pack and dug to the bottom, where he found an old T-shirt and a pair of socks. He pulled off his robe and put on the shirt before putting the robe back on again. The shirt wouldn't make much difference against the cool of the night, but it was something.

By the time he was situated, night had fallen and the last of the light faded from the sky. The stars came out in all their glory, but that was all. Carter had hoped for the moon to break the dark, but it was absent. They could see next to nothing, and the temperature was dropping by the second. With no other source of warmth, Carter moved close to Nemat and held him tight. If they were to survive together, they needed to keep each other warm. "Is this okay?" Carter asked.

"Yes," Nemat told him. Under normal circumstances, it would have been incredible to hold Nemat like this; it would have been the dream of a lifetime. But Carter was exhausted, hungry, thirsty, and scared for his life. Still, his body reacted to Nemat's closeness, his cock nestled against Nemat's butt.

"You know we can't… do that," Nemat whispered.

"My body reacts to being close to you," Carter said. "It knows what I want, and if we were in a different place, alone together, nothing could keep me from being with you the way I've dreamed of for so many weeks."

"What did you dream?" Nemat asked in a whisper that barely reached Carter's ears.

"I dreamed of you all the time," Carter answered. "Mostly they were sexy dreams about what it would like to be together." Carter swallowed, his dry throat aching. He reached for one of the nearly empty water bottles and took a sip, just enough to coat his mouth. "A couple times I dreamed of you being with me." He paused, wondering if he should go on.

"Tell me," Nemat prompted.

"After I told my family about me, I had a dream where I took you to meet them." Carter smiled. "They liked you." He rested his head against Nemat's shoulder and closed his eyes. "They were so pleased to meet you. Everyone talked and was happy. We were a family, all of us." Carter closed his eyes and let the images he remembered wash over him. "My sister Cat and her husband, Phillip, have a dog, and they had brought it with them. Why, I don't know, because that dog hates everyone but Cat, but he loved you, and the two of you ended up playing together in the backyard." It was hard for Carter to describe how bucolic the dream had been.

"It sounds like a nice dream," Nemat whispered. "Too bad it cannot be real."

Carter opened his mouth and inhaled softly before stopping the words. He wished it could be real as well. "Would you ever leave your family?" he asked cautiously. "Go live somewhere without them, I mean."

Nemat was quiet for a few seconds. "I cannot leave. They need me." He shifted on the sand. "A woman must have a male guardian. My uncle is dead, and now it is only Jalal and me. When he goes to fight, I must take care of my family." Carter felt Nemat stiffen. "That is my place and where I must always stay." Nemat's voice drifted off, and Carter handed him the bottle of water. "No matter what I want or how I feel, I must care for my family. When the war is over, I will have to find a wife and start a family. It is expected, and I do not have a choice."

"You do have a choice," Carter countered more strongly than he intended, and his throat ached from the strain.

"No. I don't have a choice. My duty is to protect and care for my family. There is nothing else I can do." Nemat turned slightly, and they moved even closer together, with Carter slightly tightening his hold. "My life has already been decided. My choices ended when my uncle was killed. Jalal is now the head of the family, and in his absence, it is me. There is no one else to care for them. There are other relatives, like Hassan, but they have their responsibilities. I cannot ask them to take on mine as well."

Carter grew quiet. "I understand."

"We should talk as little as possible," Nemat told him. Carter nodded and grew quiet as well. Nemat was right. They needed to keep as much moisture in their bodies as possible. It was also a very convenient method for shutting down a conversation that Nemat wasn't comfortable with. Carter breathed in to speak, to press Nemat, but stopped. Was it that Nemat didn't want to go with him and was using his family as an excuse not to tell him? Or was the longing he thought he heard in Nemat's voice real, and Nemat didn't want to talk any longer because the subject was too painful? Either way, the end result was the same, so it didn't matter.

The air continued to cool. Without talking, there was nothing to do but keep each other warm and wait out the night.

Carter spent some time watching the stars. Eventually he closed his eyes and leaned against Nemat, keeping his hands pressed to Nemat's skin for warmth. "It will get colder," Nemat said, and Carter nodded, trying his best to get as comfortable as possible. It wasn't easy. He felt sand and dust everywhere. When he moved, it abraded his skin, so he tried not to, but his muscles cramped, forcing him to move. The only good thing about this situation was holding Nemat, but this most certainly wasn't the way he'd been hoping to do it. But it was all he had, and cold or not, Carter began storing memories and sensations the way he would for a story, but this one would be only for him and would never be written anywhere but his heart.

After an indeterminable amount of time, Carter's teeth began to chatter. He held Nemat closer. Where they touched each other and remained close, he was warm, but the other parts of him chilled fast. They couldn't do anything about it. They simply had to make it through the night.

Carter closed his eyes and buried his face in Nemat's neck, inhaling his scent and soaking in his warmth. He tried to sleep to pass the time, even dozed off a few times, but he always woke to his teeth chattering. Hour after hour they waited. Carter listened for signs of animals or other people, but thankfully the night was quiet, and except for the now numbing cold, they seemed safe.

Never had he been so relieved to see the sky finally begin to lighten. Carter's teeth and jaw hurt from chattering. Nemat's had to hurt as well. They'd both held each other skintight all night long.

"We need to get going," Nemat told him as soon as it was light enough to see where they were going. But neither of them moved. Carter tightened his hold on Nemat, savoring a few seconds of contentment and comfort before pulling his arm from around him. Then he slowly moved away and forced himself to his feet. Nemat stood as well, opened the cooler, and gave him one of the last bottles of water. Carter drank half of it and then screwed the cap back on and placed the bottle in his pack. He handed Nemat a meal bar, and they began walking as fast as they could. Within fifteen minutes, he was no longer cold, and within an hour, the last chill of the night was long gone. Carter craved the half bottle of water in his pack, but pushed it from his mind for as long as he could.

His mouth was completely dry before he pulled out the bottle and took a shallow sip, coating his lips and throat with moisture before placing the bottle back in his pack.

The land around them changed very little, and they walked as fast as they could. Carter kept checking around them for patrols or any other threat. A few times they saw villages in the distance and altered their course to stay away from them. By afternoon, they were desperate enough for water that they went into the next town they found.

Carter waited in the shadows out of sight while Nemat went into the village. He returned a few leg-shakingly nervous minutes later with bottles of water. They both drank their fill, stowed the remaining bottles, and left town with as few people seeing them as possible. At least their thirst was quenched. Carter gave Nemat one of the meal bars from his dwindling supply—they needed energy to be able to walk.

Nemat set a fast pace. Carter managed to keep up, but just barely. He knew they would slow down as the heat of the day continued to build. He could also nearly read Nemat's mind. The prospect of spending another night out in the cold wasn't something either of them wanted to contemplate. "We should be back home by the end of the day," Nemat told him with authority.

Carter smiled and nodded. He'd be happy to be back, but that would also mean the end of the time they'd had alone. It hadn't been a picnic, by any means, but as he thought about it, he realized he'd do it all over again to be with Nemat. He blinked a few times as the thought hit home. He'd known he cared for Nemat, but somewhere over the past few days, it had grown into something more. Much more. Exactly when, he wasn't sure, but it didn't matter. When he left, he would be leaving a large part of his heart in Syria, and there wasn't a damned thing he could do about it.

He turned as someone shouted from behind them. A lone man approached them, carrying a gun. The man barked some questions Carter couldn't understand, so he glanced at Nemat. The fear he saw made his blood run cold. Nemat stopped, dropping the cooler he still carried. Carter lifted his hand and stared at the young soldier, who leveled a high-powered rifle at them. He couldn't have been much more than a child, maybe nineteen at most, but his eyes were hard as steel.

Nemat answered, and the man waved his rifle at them, moving closer. Carter had no idea what was going on, but this was not good at all. The soldier glared at them and barked what sounded like more questions. This time Carter caught enough words to know the soldier was aware they'd been to the village that had been attacked with chemical weapons. He motioned for Carter to drop his pack. Carter moved slowly, easing it off his arms and then down onto the ground.

Carter hated this. He'd spent two months immersing himself in Arabic so he could understand and speak better, but most people seemed to speak in local dialects, and he understood little more than he had on his first visit.

"Turn around," the soldier told Nemat. Carter understood the words, but didn't follow the order. Dread bloomed inside as he realized Nemat was about to be executed in front of his eyes. Carter held his breath and stared in abject horror as the soldier lifted his rifle. Carter waited until the soldier's attention faltered for a split second and then jumped him.

He expected a bang followed by pain, but instead heard a click. He slammed into the soldier, knocking him off his feet. The rifle went flying through the air and landed on the ground. The soldier was strong and pushed Carter away before leaping for his weapon. Carter wasn't sure if the weapon had jammed or if the ammunition was bad, and he didn't intend to give the soldier another chance if he could help it.

Carter grabbed for the rifle but missed it. The soldier kicked at him and caught Carter in the shoulder. Pain bloomed and traveled down his arm, but he tried again, missing the rifle for a second time. Thankfully, Nemat got to it first. He picked up the weapon, cleared the round, and then leveled the gun.

Both Carter and the child soldier stopped struggling. Carter scrambled to get away in case the soldier grabbed for him. "What do we do?" he asked and instantly swore. He'd spoken English, and he saw the soldier's eyes widen and his lips curl in abject hate. The soldier glowered at both of them. Carter had blown his cover and was in serious trouble now. The kid would report back, and people would be sent to look for him. "We need to get out of here and back to Aleppo," Carter said, hoping the city name would be understood by the soldier and cast doubt on their destination.

Nemat barked an order to the soldier and then repeated himself, louder. The kid turned around, and Nemat swung the gun like a club and hit the kid in the head. He went down like a sack of potatoes. "Dig a hole and bury this, keeping it will raise suspicion," Nemat told Carter, handing him the gun.

"Is he dead?" Carter asked. Nemat bent down, touched the man's neck, and shook his head.

"No. He'll live, but we need to go." Nemat grabbed the rifle; apparently he'd changed his mind about burying it. Carter picked up his pack and shrugged it on. Nemat grabbed the cooler, and they hurried away. After almost running a while, Nemat dropped the rifle in a small depression, kicked sand and dirt over it, and they continued their quick pace to put as much distance behind them as they could.

"Do you think there are more soldiers?" Carter asked as they moved.

"Yes. He's part of a patrol. That's why I didn't shoot him—it would make too much noise," Nemat said coldly. Carter knew it was part of the nature of war—kill or be killed—but that tone coming from Nemat sent a chill up his spine.

They continued moving at a brisk pace. Carter checked behind them every few minutes, half expecting an armored column to appear at any moment. But he didn't see anyone. He hoped the kid had been found. He hated the thought that Nemat might have killed him. He'd seen Nemat kill before, of course, but it had been from a distance, impersonal. This had been anything but. They'd looked into the soldier's eyes.

An hour passed, and then another. They had to be far enough away by now that they were out of danger, at least from the soldier and his patrol. If he wasn't dead, they might be angry, but not murderous, and hopefully their first thought was for the soldier's care rather than hunting down Nemat and Carter. They stopped to eat for a few minutes, and drink some water. Carter had just a few meal bars left now. They needed to pick up the pace or else they wouldn't get back to Nemat's family before nightfall.

"Look," Nemat said a few hours later, pointing to a hill. The sun was getting low in the sky, and Carter had started to worry. "That is near home." Nemat adjusted their course.

Carter breathed a sigh of relief, and they walked faster. The now familiar buildings got larger and more pronounced as they continued walking. An hour later, dirty, thirsty, hungry, and exhausted, they walked into Nemat's family compound just as the sun set.

CHAPTER NINE

CARTER WOKE the following day to find every muscle in his body ached. He'd slept through the pain for most of the night out of sheer exhaustion, but now he could hardly move. His legs ached from all the walking, and his shoulder throbbed where he'd been kicked. When he'd taken off his robe, he'd seen his shoulder was black and blue. How he'd worn his pack he had no idea, because now the slightest touch sent pain shooting down his arm. Thankfully, nothing seemed broken, but he had no real way to know. At least it didn't hurt as much as it had the night before, which he considered a good sign.

The other sleeping areas were empty, so Carter knew Nemat and Jalal were already up. Moving slowly and carefully, he got to his feet, holding his arm close to his body. He left the rapidly heating room and stepped out into the compound. The women were working in their cooking area, and he wandered over. They giggled as he approached. He watched them for a few minutes as they washed olives in large vats. His stomach rumbled, and one of the women, Nemat and Jalal's cousin Sabeen, if he remembered correctly, brought him a plate. She rarely smiled, not that Carter blamed her after the loss of her parents, and from what Nemat had told him briefly after they'd been introduced, her husband as well.

Carter thanked her, carried his plate to a seat in the shade, and began to eat. It would not have been appropriate for him to stay near the women without one of the men around. He wondered where

Nemat and Jalal were. He decided to try to find them once he'd eaten, but they found him as he was finishing.

"Come with me," Jalal told him in Arabic, his voice serious.

Carter nodded and returned the dishes to where the women talked and worked before following Jalal out through the olive grove to the spot where the spring bubbled from the ground. Carter eyed the cool water jealously. Jalal sat in the shade of one of the trees, and Carter gingerly sat next to him. He expected Jalal to tell him what he wanted, but Jalal sat without saying a word for a long time. Carter actually closed his eyes and enjoyed the cool air provided by the shade and water.

"Will you take Nemat with you when you go?" Jalal asked, breaking his long silence. "He should have better life than here."

This was a dream come true. Carter's heart leapt at the thought, but reality quickly set in. "I don't know if it will be that simple."

"Will your government or newspaper not want him? He can give you a lot of information. He will work hard, you know this."

"I do, and if Nemat wishes to come with me, I will take him. But he has to know that getting out of the country is only the first part." Carter paused, watching Jalal. "What brought this on?"

"I almost lost him yesterday," Jalal began, speaking slowly enough that Carter could follow his thoughts. "You saved his life again, and I thought it would be better if he went someplace where he would be safe."

"What about the rest of your family?" Carter asked.

"If I can get him out, then maybe he can help the rest of us. There is nothing here. My country is tearing apart, and though I used to think there was hope, I know now things will never be the same. My uncle is dead, and our home is destroyed for no reason. The government is in power for themselves." Jalal paused and looked at Carter, who nodded. "I want to get revenge on those who did this, but I can't. So I think about how I can make things better, and that is the way. Will you take him with you? I am asking a lot, I know."

"Yes, I'll take him with me," Carter agreed, having no idea how he was going to get Nemat into the United States, if and when he was able to get him out of Syria. "If Nemat agrees to go."

"I am the head of the family," Jalal began, but Carter raised his hand.

"This has to be what he wants. Not what you want for him," Carter explained as best he could. "I will only take him if he agrees. Nemat has the right to make his own decisions. He loves his family and his home. He took care of it as best he could while you were away." Carter didn't want to incur Jalal's wrath, but he needed him to understand. "Nemat spent time in Canada, so he knows life will be very different than he's used to. He needs to make up his mind if he's willing and able to make all the changes he will need to. You can't make that decision for someone else. Nemat must make it for himself."

Carter held out his hand and waited. He could see the indecision in Jalal's expression. Then he took Carter's hand. They had made their bargain.

"I will speak to Nemat," Jalal said. Then he stood up and walked away. Carter followed him with his eyes, wondering what he'd just agreed to. Yes, he was thrilled that Jalal wanted Nemat to go with him. The thought made his heart race. Would Nemat agree? Carter wanted to think he would, but as he'd told Jalal, that had to be Nemat's decision.

He sat in the shade for quite a while. His muscles ached, and he hoped he'd have time to heal a little before he had to travel. But he also knew that every day he stayed in the country, he put himself and Nemat and Jalal's family in danger. That thought sent a chill through him even in the oppressive heat. Nemat and his relatives were quickly becoming like a second family to him, and that was dangerous. He was here to gather information for a story. But his feelings for these people were affecting his objectivity. Even now, as he tried to think of the stories he wanted to tell, they were all from the perspective of Nemat and his family. He had to get out, gain some distance, and at the same time, ensure everyone's safety. The thought of leaving, and the possibility that

Nemat wouldn't go with him, made his heart ache. For a moment, he actually considered whether there was any way he could stay, which was ridiculous, and he shook his head at his own folly. One, two more days was all he had, and then he had to go, regardless of his aching muscles or heart.

Carter tried to clear his head of the thoughts that kept circling like vultures. He heard soft voices behind him. He turned and saw Jalal and Nemat approaching. They stopped a few feet away, talking softly but intently. Carter had a very good idea what the conversation was about, and from the body language, their discussion had just turned heated. Nemat had gone entirely rigid, arms folded across his chest as if to say, "I'm a tree, move me." He looked at Carter, eyes hard, jaw set, then turned back to Jalal. Carter looked back at the gurgling water to try to give them some privacy.

The two of them talked for quite a while, and then Carter heard them approach. He didn't turn to watch, but let them come on their own.

"Did you convince Jalal that I should go with you?" Nemat asked, standing in front of him with the same hard expression Carter had seen earlier.

"No. He asked me if I'd take you with me," Carter explained. Nemat's expression softened slightly. Apparently that meshed with what Jalal had told him. The two brothers had another heated discussion, and Carter didn't try to follow it. They needed to talk and come to a decision. As much as Carter wanted Nemat to come with him, to be away from this place and to possibly have a life with him, he needed to stay out of it. His heart told him, well, actually, it screamed at him to beg Nemat to come with him, but he kept quiet.

Eventually the discussion ended. Both brothers stared at each other, arms held defiantly. Carter moved his attention from Nemat to Jalal and then back again, waiting for some sort of answer.

"He goes with you," Jalal ordered and then turned and strode away. "No more argument."

Carter waited until Jalal was gone and then motioned for Nemat to sit down. "I told him that leaving had to be your decision. He can't make it for you. You need to decide what you want."

Nemat sat without answering for a long time. Carter had learned enough about the strong, kind, and deliberate man to let him work through what he needed.

"I want to do what's best for the family. Jalal says that is me leaving with you. But how can that be?" Nemat finally asked.

"I think Jalal is trying to think long-term," Carter began and then lost track of his thought. "I will not influence your decision or make it for you. If you decide to stay, then you stay. I want to make sure you understand that. No matter what Jalal says, you make this decision yourself. I can tell you what I think, and so can Jalal, but it's what you want that counts. Okay?"

Nemat nodded slowly.

"You must say you understand," Carter said. He knew he was talking quickly, and he took a deep breath to slow his speech.

"Yes. I understand."

"Okay. Maybe Jalal is thinking of your family when he says he wants you to go. You are part of his family, and he told me he wants a better life for you." Carter paused, and Nemat looked back toward what was left of the house. "I also have to tell you that there are no guarantees that once we get out of the country you'll be able to get into the United States. I'm no expert on such things, but it can be difficult." Carter thought about the phone number he'd memorized and wondered if the people who answered that telephone could provide assistance.

"What would happen if I cannot get into your country?" Nemat asked softly.

"Then you would need to cross back into Syria, or you could try to stay in Turkey. I believe the difficult part will be getting out. There are more patrols and guards at the borders. It wasn't difficult for me to cross with the refugees the last time, but I don't know if we can do the same thing now. We might need to get creative." Carter paused. "No one looked at me twice the last time because there were so many people. But with the two of us together, especially two men, we could raise suspicion that we're fighters." Carter's head began to swim a little, and he closed his eyes. "I find it hard to predict anything. The fighting rages, people cross the border to get away, and then come back only to leave again."

"You don't sound convincing," Nemat told him.

Carter shifted, mindful of his shoulder. "I want you to come with me. I really do," he whispered. "I hate the thought of you being in danger." He looked toward the house. "The attack that killed some of your family could have killed you too. That thought fills me with dread." He had to keep from reaching for Nemat. He desperately wanted to pull Nemat to him and hold him for all he was worth. "But like I told Jalal, it has to be your decision. I can guarantee it won't be easy, and there will be disappointments and setbacks. We might not be able to get out of Syria, and if we do, you might not be allowed into the United States. But there is a chance, and I'm willing to help if you want to take it."

"Where would I live?"

Carter wanted to offer that he could live with him, but wondered if that would be presuming too much. If Nemat came with him, he'd have to be able to choose the way he wanted to live his life. Carter was one of the few gay people Nemat had ever known other than himself. While Carter knew what he wanted, he needed to give Nemat the chance to make up his own mind. "I have a small apartment in New York, and you can live there. As for work, you'd probably do very well as a mechanic. There are plenty of cars that need to be fixed." He paused. "I'll need to leave in two days at the latest. The longer I'm here, the more danger your family is in. Friends and neighbors will become suspicious of the stranger staying with you."

Nemat nodded, appearing pensive.

Carter had done his best to stay out of sight, wearing only local clothing and trying to blend in. But it would only take so long before others became suspicious, especially at a time when the entire country seemed on the verge of a nervous breakdown. "Let me know tomorrow what you decide, and don't worry about what Jalal thinks. You have to do what you think is right."

Nemat chewed on his lower lip. "He is the head of the family."

"Up until a few days ago, that was your role. You took care of your family and saw them through tough times. You earned the right to make your own decisions. Jalal knows that. He only wants what he sees as best for you." Carter wanted the exact same thing. Looking into Nemat's eyes, he wondered what he would decide. He hoped for some sort of clue, but none was forthcoming. He did see confusion and doubt in Nemat's deep chocolate eyes. Carter wanted to soothe it all away, but that seemed impossible.

"I have work to do," Nemat told him before standing up and turning to leave.

Carter watched him hurry away and then lowered his gaze in case anyone was watching. He shifted, watching the water. He knew he should be getting his things together and making plans to leave, but he couldn't bring himself to do it. He hoped Nemat would decide to go with him, but it was a huge risk for him. Carter was sure they could get out of Syria somehow. He began running through scenarios in his mind, and it wasn't long before his jaw dropped open, the full realization of what Nemat was being asked to do settling on him. No wonder Nemat was hesitant. He was being asked to give up everything he'd ever known. His entire world would change if he left. Nemat would be leaving his family and friends to travel to a new place where the only person he knew was Carter. Yes, Carter wanted Nemat to come with him, but had he given him a reason to make that choice? He'd said the decision was Nemat's, and it had to be, but how could he possibly decide to go when there was no real reason for him to go?

He stared at the crystal-clear water as it wound its way across the otherwise parched ground toward its eventual demise back into the desert. When he'd left the last time, Carter had promised Nemat that he'd never forget him. He hadn't lied. But he also hadn't said what was in his heart. He carefully got to his feet, deciding that should change. If Nemat was to decide about going with him, then he deserved to know everything, including how Carter felt about him. He strode back toward the compound, looking in each of the buildings.

He found Nemat bent over the engine of the truck. The sight nearly took his breath away, and he had to keep from gasping openly. Nemat continued working, obviously unaware that he was there. Carter cleared his throat, and Nemat looked up from his work, nearly hitting his head on the open hood. "I didn't mean to startle you," Carter said, moving closer. "Can I talk to you?"

Nemat wiped his hands on an old cloth after straightening up. Carter opened his mouth to say what he desperately wanted to say. Nemat looked at him, his eyes warm, lips slightly parted, almost inviting him to taste. The words were on the very tip of Carter's tongue... and he couldn't say them. He wanted to more than anything in the world, but it wasn't fair to Nemat. Carter could tell Nemat how he felt, but then he'd always wonder if that was the reason Nemat had left his home, his family, and everything he knew. A few seconds earlier, he'd been so eager to tell him just how he felt, but he realized he couldn't do it. If Nemat came with him, it had to be his decision and only his. That was what Carter had promised.

"Did you want something?" Nemat asked.

Carter sighed and closed his mouth. "No, I'm sorry," he said before he turned and hurried away. He felt like a total idiot. Yes, he wanted Nemat to know how he felt, but he should have told him before now. He should have said something when they were both freezing in the desert, because even as cold as it had gotten, the memory of being able to hold Nemat the entire night was more powerful than that of the cold. He knew that in time how cold it had been would completely fade, but the memory of having Nemat in his arms, the way he felt—firm and warm in the cold air, his scent, musky and rich, and especially the way he trembled when he'd realized what was pressing against his butt—those sensations would stay with Carter until he died. He returned to the spring and sat back down near the running water.

CARTER SPENT much of the rest of the day sitting alone. That night he gingerly tossed and turned, trying to find a comfortable position. Eventually, he fell asleep. His shoulder felt somewhat better the following morning. His arm ached much less, and while it still felt stiff, he was now sure it wasn't broken, which was a relief. He spent part of the day with Nemat, helping him with his chores. Carter kept waiting for him to say something about what he'd decided, but Nemat kept that information to himself.

Dinner that evening was quiet. The tension between Jalal and Nemat was so strong that the air sizzled with it. The women usually whispered among themselves, but they were stone quiet as well. Every time Carter lifted his gaze, they seemed to shy away. Once the meal was over, Carter thanked his hosts and hostesses for their hospitality and left the communal room. He walked across the compound and entered the small room where he'd slept since he'd arrived. He got his pack and went through it, making sure he had all his notes as well as the pieces of shell casing. He desperately wanted them to contain the proof he needed, but he wouldn't know until he could get them tested. He stared at the bits of brass and hoped like hell they could be used to prove what he knew in his heart had happened in that small village.

He placed the plastic bags in the bottom of his pack, along with his notebooks. Then he added a layer of clothes before putting in the last two meal bars he had. His phone went in next, and then he added more clothes. He'd decided to leave the rest. When he was done, Carter pulled open the door and sat in the doorway, staring out over the compound. Sure, the main house had been destroyed, but Nemat and his family carried on with what they had. They made do and were still living their lives. They were resilient and defiant in the face of what would have broken most people.

"Carter," Nemat said softly as he approached. Carter slid over, and Nemat sat next to him. "I cannot go with you."

Carter wasn't surprised. That tension at dinner had to be because Nemat and Jalal had disagreed. "It's your decision," he said, trying not to let his disappointment show. Still he swallowed hard and waited for him to continue.

"I can't leave my family alone. They need me," Nemat said, but he refused to look at him. Carter knew in his heart that Nemat wasn't telling him the whole truth.

"You told Jalal already," Carter supplied, and Nemat nodded.

"He was angry with me. He told me I was throwing away the chance of a lifetime. He said I could have a better life and that I was spitting in his face."

"Nemat," Jalal called sharply. Nemat stood up and walked over to where his brother stood. Carter glanced at them and then turned away. Rather than what they said, he heard the tone in their voices. This was definitely not a pleasant conversation. Their voices rose, growing louder, with shouts and curses flying back and forth. Then suddenly Nemat whirled on his heels and stalked off. Carter waited for Nemat to return, but Jalal raced back to his brother, grabbing his shoulders. Carter was afraid Jalal was going to shake Nemat, but instead, he pulled his brother into his arms and hugged him tightly. They stayed that way for a long while. Carter thought he saw Jalal's lips moving slightly, but he wasn't sure. He stood up and went inside. He felt like he was watching something private and it felt wrong to him.

He stayed inside until he heard footsteps, and then Nemat stepped inside. Carter pretended to be busy looking inside his pack. "I will go with you," Nemat said softly.

Carter wanted to ask him why he'd had the change of heart, but he had a pretty good idea that instead of yelling, Nemat's big brother had appealed to his heart. "Okay. We need to pack for a long walk. Hopefully this time we can avoid getting shelled and having someone point a gun at us. All we need to do is walk north, and we'll cross the border close to where I entered the country. Once we're out of Syria, I'll make a few phone calls, and we should have some help." At least he hoped so.

"What will happen then?" Nemat asked.

"You need to get your identity papers and any other identification you have. We'll make our way to Istanbul and then figure things out." He wished he had more information or could offer more hope. But he really didn't know. All he was sure of was that Nemat was going to come with him. "You and your brother took care of me and had my back more than once. When we leave, it'll be my turn," Carter said.

"Okay, I trust you," Nemat told him and then smiled slightly.

"Pack only what you can carry," Carter said. Nemat nodded, and Carter dug his phone out of his pack and left the room. There was just enough light, so Carter walked around the compound, taking pictures of the buildings. He snapped a shot of Jalal and the women as they worked, knowing Nemat would miss all of them.

Then he stepped out into the olive grove and took pictures of the trees and sky. Finally, he made his way to the spring and took some pictures of the water and greenery surrounded by the starker desert. By the time he was done, the light was fading. He walked back to the compound.

As the last of the light faded, Carter sat on a rough bench outside the shed where he'd slept. No one else was about, but voices, some filled with tears, others laughter, drifted from the other building. Nemat's voice reached his ears, bursting with emotion. Jalal's as well. Carter closed his eyes and wondered just how you said good-bye to people you loved, whom you'd fought for, cared deeply for, when you might never see them again. He knew that happened when someone died, but this was different. Every person in the small building knew they might never see or hear from Nemat again. How do you say good-bye? What do you say? Carter thought about his parents and what he'd say to them in that situation, and he realized he'd be at a total loss for words, something very rare, given his profession.

Carter sat alone, giving them their time as a family. Laughter drifted through the air. It started softly and then quickly built as what sounded like all of Nemat's family joined in. He realized they were most likely sharing stories, memories of their times together, reinforcing their bond. It didn't matter what the stories were, because every family had them—as long as they all remembered, they would be a family. Carter blinked a few times and then wiped his eyes.

The laughter died away, and Carter heard little more for a while. Then the laughter began again before dying away once more. Carter couldn't make out what they were saying, and he didn't really want to. These were their memories and stories, and they had to remain so. Eventually, more serious voices drifted to his ears, followed by what he was certain were sobs. The timbre and cadence of Jalal's voice carried to Carter's ears. He wondered what one brother said to another at a time like this. What would Carter have said to his sister? How do you say thank you for a lifetime of friendship, fights, support, arguments, and always knowing who had your back, no matter what? He inhaled deeply and then sighed softly before standing up and going inside. The night chill was setting in. He closed the door and made up the beds before lying down and staring up at the ceiling. No way would he interrupt them. They needed and deserved their time alone.

How long he lay there, Carter didn't know. Eventually, he dozed off for a while, but woke when the door opened. Nemat stepped inside. It was nearly pitch dark, but in the little light that filtered in from outside, Carter saw Nemat wipe his eyes. He remained still. While Carter wanted to provide comfort, he couldn't; it wasn't safe, so he thought it best to pretend to be asleep.

"I know you're not asleep," Nemat said softly. Carter stretched and slowly sat up. "I am ready to go."

"Nemat," Carter began, tempted to pull him into his arms.

"There is nothing you can do," Nemat whispered. "I have made up my mind, and I will go with you."

Carter nodded in the darkness. "Where's Jalal?"

"Thinking," Nemat said. He moved through the room, and Carter saw his dark form descend onto his bed. "We will have a lot of walking tomorrow."

"Yes," Carter agreed, carefully turning onto his side. "I've been thinking, too, and while going cross-country would probably be safer, I think we need to cross at the official border."

"Why?"

"It would be better if you went into Turkey legally rather than sneaking across the border. It might make it easier to get you into the United States. I don't know, but I think even though it's more dangerous for me, it would give you more opportunities."

"You did it before," Nemat said.

"Yes, but the last report I heard said the government controlled that area now. It was out of government hands when I crossed last time. I don't know what we'll encounter, or if the border will even be open. But I think you need to make the official entry into Turkey. Otherwise you'll be in Turkey illegally, and they might send you back." The thought of making it that far and then having Nemat sent back was almost too much to think about. "We'll do everything we can as officially as possible."

Nemat stood up, and Carter heard the soft scuff as he slipped into his shoes. "I will ask Jalal to drive us as close he can." Nemat left the room, and Carter lay quietly, listening. After a while he heard footsteps outside the door, and then both brothers came inside.

"I will take you," Jalal said. The brothers both lay down, and the room became quiet, with only the soft breathing of Carter's companions to break the sounds of the night. Carter knew none of them would get much sleep. How could they?

CHAPTER
TEN

CARTER MUST have fallen to sleep at some point, because he jolted awake when the door opened and light streamed into the room. Nemat stepped in, his hair still wet. Carter looked to Jalal's bed and saw it was empty. Then he looked back at Nemat, smiling at the sight in front of him. He took a deep breath and looked away when he heard Jalal outside.

"Bathe quickly, and we will get ready to go," Nemat said firmly. Carter didn't argue. He picked up the clothes he intended to wear and headed down to the spring.

He was alone, and the water was bracing as he washed himself quickly. The parched air was already warming, and it quickly dried his skin. Carter dressed and strode back to the compound. He got his pack and found Nemat and Jalal by the truck, the driver's door standing open. Carter placed his pack inside and turned to Jalal.

"Take care of him," Jalal said as a huge lump formed in Carter's throat.

"I will, I promise," Carter said. "You take care of the family." Jalal nodded, and Carter pulled him into a hug. "You have done great things for me. I never had a brother before."

"Now I have two," Jalal whispered, and Carter's eyes watered. They parted, and Carter walked around the truck. He climbed in, and Nemat got in on the other side and scooted to the center of the bench seat. Jalal got in the truck as well, and pulled his door closed. They rolled down the windows, and Jalal started the engine. The women stood nearby, and all three of them waved. They waved back, and

Carter saw Nemat's lip tremble slightly. Then Jalal pulled away and out onto the road.

No one spoke much. Carter stared out the windows, looking for any sign of danger, and Nemat watched his home disappear behind them.

"It's for the best," Jalal said, and Nemat shrugged without arguing or agreeing. They followed the same route Nemat had taken Carter the last time he'd left the country. But it was different this time. They saw very few other vehicles. Jalal turned toward the border, and they encountered a few people walking north, but not the large groups Carter had been able to mingle among.

"You probably shouldn't go much farther," Carter said. Jalal drove a little ways, cresting a small rise. The road stretched out in front of the truck. Carter saw a few people heading toward the border, so he hoped it was still open. In the distance, he could see what appeared to be the actual crossing. Jalal pulled to a stop, and Carter opened his door and pulled out his beat-up pack. "Thank you," he said to Jalal and then stepped away from the truck so Nemat and Jalal could have a few minutes. When Nemat joined him, they watched as Jalal turned his body and waved before he turned the truck around, drove over the top of the rise, and disappeared from sight.

"No English," Nemat said softly, and Carter nodded. He started walking. It took a few seconds before he realized Nemat wasn't with him. He turned and saw Nemat looking for something in his duffel bag. Carter waited, and Nemat pulled out some papers, closed the duffel, and hurried to where Carter stood. "Use these," Nemat said, stuffing the papers in his hand. "You remember Ashur?" Nemat said, and Carter nodded. He was one of the men from the brigade. Carter remembered his quiet demeanor and ready smile.

Carter took the papers, knowing what it meant: Ashur hadn't made it. Carter blinked a few times and then turned away, holding tightly to the dead man's identity papers. He couldn't read them, of course, and the picture was grainy, but it did look somewhat like him. There was no way it would pass a close inspection, though. Hopefully it was close enough that he could slip through. Carter didn't move and said a quiet thank-you to Ashur before turning to Nemat.

They started walking. Carter had made up a rudimentary sling for his arm, and when the aching started, he put it on, hoping he appeared unthreatening and relatively helpless. He hoped it would make the border guards less likely to pay much attention to him. They didn't rush and shuffled slightly as they walked. The number of people thickened a little as they got closer to the crossing. On their side, soldiers with guns stood at a checkpoint. Carter craned his neck to see people slowly passing in front of them. The line moved very slowly.

As they got closer, one of the guards stepped forward and pulled a man and woman out of line, then jerked the coverings off their heads. He yanked them off to the side toward a waiting truck. Nemat gasped slightly, and Carter swallowed his horror, looking away as first the woman and then the man were physically tossed into the back of the truck. Some of the people in line calmly stepped out and began to slowly walk away from the border, mixing in with the people crossing back from Turkey. He wanted to ask what that was about and what they'd done, but Nemat moved closer and lowered his eyes, so Carter did the same.

His heart beat a staccato in his ears as he and Nemat approached the crossing. People held out their papers for the guards, who barely seemed to look at them. Carter noticed that the guards were watching people's feet. He glanced down at his own shoes, still caked in dirt and dust from the earlier trek across the desert as well as their walk today.

Carter held his breath as he approached the crossing itself. He stepped in front of the guard and heard a shout. Carter braced as the guard yelled again. He stopped and glanced upward. The man in front of him took to his heels, racing the final few feet toward the border. The guard yelled again, and then the sound of rapid gunfire split the air. Carter fell to the ground, hoping like hell he or Nemat didn't get hit. Once the gunfire stopped, Carter lifted his head and inched forward. "Go," Nemat whispered, and Carter continued moving forward, crawling across the checkpoint.

Guards moved on either side of them, but no one paid attention to him or Nemat. He stood up and walked the short distance to the

Turkish checkpoint, letting Nemat go first. Once he was across, Carter opened the outside compartment of his pack and fished his US passport out of the hidden compartment. The Turkish guard's eyes widened. He examined it carefully and then motioned Carter across the border. They'd made it. They were out.

Carter and Nemat moved away from the crossing. Carter pulled his phone out of the pack. He managed to get a satellite signal and dialed the memorized number.

"Yes."

"I'm Carter Hopkins. Agent Dempsey gave me this number," Carter said, unsure of the protocol. The line went quiet, and after about thirty seconds, the man returned. "We see where you are."

"Good. I have information you might be interested in. I want to speak to Agent Dempsey in Istanbul tomorrow. I also need some help with transportation." Carter was about to hang up, but then said, "Also, please tell him that I have one of the sources with me who he might wish to speak with."

"We'll be in touch," the voice said, and the line went dead. Carter and Nemat continued farther into Turkey. Carter wasn't sure exactly what he should do. In one direction was the refugee camp, in the other basically open space. He thought about calling Olivier to see if he could arrange transportation while he waited to hear back. He was about to make the call when his phone rang.

"A car is on its way."

The line went dead again, and Carter put the phone away. Why couldn't these people act like regular human beings? A few minutes later, a black sedan pulled up. The driver got out and walked up to them. "Mr. Hopkins," he said and ushered them toward the car. With nothing to lose, Carter motioned Nemat forward, and they got inside. The air conditioning felt amazing, and he slumped in the seat.

"Where are we going?" Nemat asked, his eyes wide. "Am I a prisoner?"

Carter paused. "No. They're giving us a ride. Isn't that right?" he asked the driver.

"Yes. I've been instructed to take you to Istanbul. We have a hotel room for you, and Dempsey will meet you there."

"What's going on?" Nemat asked with a touch of fear.

"When I got back, I met with a federal agent, and he gave me a number to call if I needed some help. They're going to take us to a hotel and hopefully help you come with me." As they rode, Carter wondered just what kind of game he'd started. Carter was pretty sure he had something they'd want, and he was hoping to use that to get what he wanted. He moved closer to Nemat and put his arm around him. "It's going to be fine."

The ride took hours, but soon they were back in the shadow of Hagia Sophia. The car pulled under the portico of a nice chain hotel, and they got out and went inside the lobby, where they found Agent Dempsey waiting for them.

"How did...." Carter had started to ask how Agent Dempsey had gotten here so fast, but knew he'd never tell him.

"We have a room for you, and we need to talk," Agent Dempsey said, leading them toward the elevator.

Carter could feel the tension rolling off Nemat. "It's okay," he soothed.

"What if they send me back?" Nemat asked.

"That's what we're trying to prevent," Carter told him. They entered the hotel room. Nemat stepped inside and looked all around.

"You called us, Mr. Hopkins," Agent Dempsey said. "You said you had something we might want."

"Yes." Carter set down his pack and dug to the bottom, then pulled out one of the shell fragments. He handed it to the agent. "This was taken from a village that was rumored to have been gassed. Have it tested, because it could prove the use of chemical weapons. We almost died getting away when the town was shelled into oblivion. I can give you the GPS coordinates as well."

"What do you want in return?"

"I want Nemat, here, allowed into the US," Carter said.

"I can't do that," Dempsey said.

Carter snatched the plastic bag from the agent's hand. "Then you get nothing. Thanks for the ride. I'll contact my paper and begin writing my story. You can read the details along with the rest of the world and try to figure out exactly where the village is."

"How do we know he isn't a member of a terrorist organization?" Dempsey asked.

"Because this man and his family have been fighting their own government. They took me in and helped me find the mass grave as well as possible proof that the Syrian government is using chemical weapons on its own people. You know that proof will turn Syria's last allies against them. There are lines even they won't cross." Carter stepped closer to the agent. "I can give you the proof, but I want him given a green card and allowed into the United States."

"Why?" Dempsey asked as he looked at Nemat and then back at Carter.

"I have my reasons," Carter said. "He and his family took care of me, and now it's my turn to take care of him."

"I'll have to make some phone calls," Dempsey said.

"Call whoever you need. But I can tell from the way you're trying not to look interested that you can taste what I'm willing to give you. So make your calls." Carter wasn't about to back down. He knew they wanted what he had. Rumors of the use of chemical weapons had been all over the news before he left, but they'd been just that—rumors. Carter watched the agent speaking softly into his phone.

"Why are you doing this? You got everything, and you gave it to him. Why?" Nemat asked in a whisper.

"For you," Carter answered. "I'll give them what I know they want so you can come to the United States." It might cost him his job, but Nemat was more important. Nemat inhaled sharply, and Carter reached for his hand. "I mean it. There are all kinds of rules about who can get into the country, and it was the only way I could think of to get past those rules."

Agent Dempsey returned, talking softly before hanging up his phone. "I need to speak with him," he said.

"His name is Nemat," Carter said.

"I'd need to speak to Nemat, but if your information checks out and he doesn't pose a threat, then we have a deal," Agent Dempsey told them. "But you can't write about any of this."

Carter paused. "I'll write my story about what I found. Our conversation here will be considered off the record, as will any arrangement made for Nemat, but everything else will be included."

Agent Dempsey paused and then nodded. "Fair enough."

Carter handed the agent the casings, and Agent Dempsey turned toward the door. "Just one more thing," Carter said. "If I find out the room has been wired, either video or audio, the deal is off, and everything, every conversation we've ever had, will be considered on the record."

Dempsey didn't falter for a second. "The room is clean." He opened the door and left. Carter followed and locked the door.

"Why did you do all that?" Nemat asked. "Why did you give him anything?"

"Because you came with me," Carter said. "When I left the last time, I was heartsick. I thought about you all the time." He slowly stepped toward Nemat. "I wondered the entire time I was gone if you were all right. I dreamed about you."

"Why?"

"Because I love you, Nemat," Carter said. "I wanted to tell you before, but I didn't want that to be the reason you came with me."

"But it is. I came because I love you too. But I wasn't sure if that was more important than my family. I was always taught that kind of"—Nemat swallowed—"love was wrong. How could something wrong be more important than what my family needed?"

"Does how you feel really seem wrong to you?" Carter asked, stepping closer. He reached out and stroked Nemat's cheek. "Does this feel wrong?" He leaned forward, guiding their lips together. Their kiss began soft and gentle, then progressed slowly through firm to deep and then urgent. Carter held Nemat to him, needing to feel him from lips to toes. "You taste so good," he whispered after gasping for breath. He kissed Nemat again, pressing him back through the room and then down onto the huge bed.

They fell together. Carter sighed as the soft mattress cushioned their descent.

"What was that for?" Nemat asked.

"No more sleeping on the floor," Carter said, rolling Nemat onto his back. He reached for the hem of Nemat's robe and pulled at the fabric until he was able to get it up and eventually off. Nemat wasn't as gentle. He did manage to get Carter's robe off as well, but Carter heard the sound of ripping fabric and stitches. Carter positioned Nemat on the bed and stretched out on top of him, staring down into his deep, dark eyes. "You are so beautiful. There have been so many things I've wanted to tell you."

"Like what?" Nemat asked.

"That the first time I saw you, I could barely see straight. Remember? The area that had once been a market outside Aleppo. I approached Jalal and gave him the message I'd been told to pass to him. You stayed undercover, watching his back. I remember when he motioned and you first stepped out from behind that wall."

"You knew I was...."

"The word is gay, and no, but your eyes drew me in within seconds. I didn't dare stare at you too long, but I wanted to. After that I kept an eye on you; thankfully, no one noticed. It took me a few days before I saw that you were watching me too." Carter lightly stroked Nemat's cheek and then kissed him gently. His body throbbed with excitement, but they'd waited this long.... He and Nemat were in a hotel, behind a locked door. Now he could take his time and say the things he'd wanted to.

"Then after we spent that night alone in Aleppo, you were all I could think about." Carter kissed Nemat hard, energy shooting between them like an electric charge. Talking became secondary, and the things he wanted to say flew from his head when Nemat moaned. That tiny sound sent a ripple through him that built into a tsunami of need. Carter kissed him again and then lightly kissed his way down Nemat's neck. He found a spot, right at the base of his throat. When he touched it, Nemat writhed and moaned louder. God, that sound was beautiful and so liberating. They'd always had to be stone quiet whenever they were together. He'd never realized just how important the sounds of love actually were.

"Carter," Nemat whispered.

"You don't have to be quiet. You can make all the sound you want," Carter whispered, and then he licked over one of Nemat's brown nipples. Nemat groaned, and Carter did it again. "Yes."

Carter adored the taste of Nemat's skin. He trailed his tongue over his chest, then licked and sucked his nipples to nubs before sitting back.

"What?"

"I'm looking at you. I never got to really see you before." He stared at Nemat's light-brown skin, wisps of dark hair between his pecs, and the trail that led to his cock, which throbbed under Carter's attention. He was so tempted to dive right in. Nemat squirmed, and Carter smiled, then slowly ran his hands up Nemat's belly and chest, over his shoulders, and down his arms to his hands before entwining their fingers. "You are an amazing man."

"No, I'm not," Nemat countered.

"Yes, you are. You're patient and kind, strong when you need to be, and always willing to put others first. Why do you think Jalal kept insisting you come with me? He knew you'd never ask on your own. You'd stay with your family and hide who you really were forever."

Nemat gasped. "Did he know?"

"No," Carter soothed. "I don't think so. He wanted more for you." He closed his eyes, thanking his lucky stars and everything that was great and good that Nemat had indeed changed his mind. He slowly lowered himself onto Nemat's warm body, holding him tight as every warm, radiant sensation sent a thrill through him. They kissed, and Carter rolled them on the bed until Nemat pressed him into the mattress. He wasn't sure how Nemat would feel regarding positions during lovemaking, and Carter was versatile, so he figured he'd let Nemat call the shots.

What he should have remembered was Nemat's inexperience. Nemat kissed him but seemed prepared to go no further. "Is this okay?"

"Do what you think feels good," Carter whispered, and Nemat licked his neck and then down to his nipples, mimicking what Carter had done. As Nemat moved lower, Carter held his breath. When he felt Nemat's hot breath on his cock, he closed his eyes, afraid to move, willing Nemat to go further. Intense heat surrounded him. He groaned softly from deep in his throat, and Nemat took him deeper. "Go slow," he said softly.

Nemat took him deeper, sucking lightly at first, slowly growing more and more powerful. Carter breathed deeply, gasping at the intensity. His heart beat a mile a minute, and he fisted the bedding in an effort to keep from thrusting. He wanted more, but was not willing to simply take it. "Yes," he whispered. "That's so good."

He lifted his head, watching as his cock slipped from between Nemat's lips. That sight alone nearly sent him over the edge. His eyes crossed when Nemat took him deeper, sucking hard before releasing him. Carter gasped for air and to retain control of his body, which was quickly developing a mind of its own.

"Is this okay?" Nemat asked after Carter's cock slipped from his mouth.

"Oh God, yes," Carter said. He cupped Nemat's cheeks and guided him upward until their mouths met. The kiss was searing, and Carter wrapped his legs around Nemat's waist in a silent invitation.

Nemat seemed hesitant at first, most likely unsure if he understood what Carter wanted. But soon he grew bolder. Carter wished he'd brought supplies, and realized what he really wanted would have to wait until another time. He groaned his frustration and then deepened the kiss so Nemat didn't think he'd done anything wrong. They kissed hard, and Carter kept his arms and legs wrapped around Nemat as Nemat thrust slowly. Nemat's cock slid past Carter's, and with every stroke, a zing of pleasure shot through him.

They moved together, Carter easily shifting his movements to coincide with Nemat's. The moans and whimpers increased. Nemat chanted just under his breath. Carter didn't understand him, but he had an idea what Nemat was saying. Those sorts of things were easily communicated, no matter what the language. Between Nemat's moans and his own whimpers, he knew they were both getting close. Tingling started in Carter's balls and quickly spread throughout his body. He heard Nemat groan and felt him still. Soon heat spread between them. That snapped the last of Carter's control and he came, seeing stars behind his eyes.

Carter stilled, holding Nemat tight as he floated on clouds of happiness. For the past week he'd been on edge almost every second, but now they were out and together. He held his breath and almost instantly descended back to earth as he realized he'd never asked Nemat what he wanted. He'd simply assumed that once they'd gotten out Nemat would want to be with him. What if he'd been wrong? Nemat still deserved the chance to make his own decisions.

Carter had insisted on that when Jalal had wanted to make Nemat's decisions for him. He had to be prepared to do the same.

"What happens now?" Nemat asked. Carter held him, breathing deeply and trying not to let his worries run away with him.

"Well, we wait to see what Agent Dempsey returns with. Once we get his answer, we'll go from there." Carter checked the time and did a quick calculation. He'd call his family and the paper later that evening and let them know he was out and safe. He wasn't in too big a hurry, and he'd rather know where he stood before he made himself known. "I need to get my equipment from my contact and start working on my stories. Then hopefully we can get on a plane and begin our journey home."

Nemat turned away from him. "Where will I live?" he asked. "You said I could live with you if I wanted. Are we still doing that?"

Carter lifted Nemat's chin. "You get to choose what you want. You can live with me, most definitely." He swallowed hard. "You can also find a place of your own."

"I don't understand," Nemat said. "I thought you wanted me."

Carter sighed. "Of course I do. But just like I told Jalal that he had to let you decide, I have to let you choose your life. I didn't want to presume that you'd want to come live with me." He blinked at the confusion in Nemat's eyes. "You get to make your own decisions now. When we get to New York, you can live as a gay man if that's what you want. There are places to go where you can meet other men like us. Clubs where men meet and dance and talk." He took a deep breath. "You might meet someone you like better."

Nemat's expression clouded. Carter tried to read it, but couldn't. Finally Nemat shook his head. "You're teasing me."

"You've only met me. What if…." Carter shifted nervously. "You deserve the chance to make sure I'm the person you want to be with." Carter knew his own mind and heart. Nemat deserved the chance to know his own as well.

"Do you think I'm stupid?" Nemat asked. "That I don't know my own head?" He shifted and moved away on the bed. "I can make up my own mind just fine."

"I didn't…," Carter began.

Nemat interrupted him. "I know what I want."

"But what if you change your mind? New York is very different from everything you know. People will accept that you're gay. I'll introduce you to other couples, because I do want you—I love you. But I don't want to trap you into a relationship, either."

Nemat nodded. "You met my grandmother." Carter nodded. "She and my grandfather were married because their fathers thought they would be a good match."

"Were they?" Carter asked.

"Yes. But Grandma told me she didn't want to marry him. She was in love with another boy from the village and wanted to marry him. Her father said no, and she married Grandfather." Nemat paused, and Carter wondered what point he was trying to make, but kept quiet and let him finish. "She told me that she was wrong. The boy she was in love with married another woman and used to beat his wife all the time. Grandma told me that she grew to love Grandfather very deeply. He was a good man who loved her and wasn't afraid to show it. Grandma smiled when she told me that part. She also told me there are no guarantees in life or love. They were happy together until my grandfather died."

Carter still didn't get the point of the story and hoped Nemat would explain it to him.

"Grandma always said to choose who you love carefully, and she was right." Nemat shifted on the bed. "I choose you. So I don't need these places where men go to meet, and I don't need to bed a lot of other men." Nemat smiled brilliantly. "I think I would like to go dancing. I bet it's very different from the kind of dancing I'm used to."

"If you're sure," Carter said.

Nemat snuggled a little closer. "That you would be concerned about such things does you great credit." Nemat kissed him and closed his eyes. They were both exhausted. Carter held Nemat, closed his eyes, and quickly fell asleep.

He didn't stay that way for long. His phone rang, and he groaned, rolling over on the bed. He got up and searched through his things for his phone, answering it just before the call went to voice mail.

"This is Dempsey. I'm on my way back. We need to talk."

"Okay," Carter said softly.

"I'll be up in five minutes. If that's okay."

Carter actually paused at the politeness. "We're just taking a nap. It's been a long couple days. See you then." Carter hung up, and his heart raced as he wondered about the news. He woke Nemat, and they cleaned up and dressed quickly and were sitting on the small sofa when a knock sounded on the door. Carter peered through the peephole and then opened the door to the agent, who strode inside. Carter closed the door and joined Nemat.

"The sample tested positive for remnants of chemical agents," Dempsey told them. Carter nodded and waited for more. "Do you have others?"

"I won't tell you that," Carter said. "I've given you proof of what I found, and I'll give you the location in question, but you know my terms."

"I could have you arrested for collaborating with the enemy," Dempsey said sternly.

"You could try. Word would get out you locked up a reporter, and you know things like that don't stay secret for long," Carter countered, even as worry bloomed in his stomach.

Dempsey shook his head and then looked at Nemat before returning his attention to Carter. "I need to speak to him."

Carter turned to Nemat. "You don't have to," he told Nemat and then turned back to Dempsey once Nemat had agreed. "I'm staying here." He sat next to Nemat and dared the agent to try and stop him.

"You aren't scared of anything, are you?" Dempsey asked.

"After what he and I've seen, it would take more than you to scare us," Carter answered and motioned toward a chair. Dempsey sat down and spent the next hour or so asking Nemat questions about his life, from where he was born to religious beliefs and his opinion of the US and members of its government. Nemat told him about his time as a freedom fighter and the things he'd seen and done. Nemat described seeing the bodies of women and children after attacks and about first finding the mass grave, purely by accident and only because of the shifting sand and wind.

"Where is your family now?" Agent Dempsey asked.

"What's left of my family is living on our land," Nemat answered. "My brother was a freedom fighter as well, but now he cares for the family."

Carter looked back and forth between the agent and Nemat.

"Have you been to his family home?" Agent Dempsey asked Carter, who nodded.

"I know his brother, and I knew his uncle before he was killed. I know you're nervous about granting what I'm asking, but it's because of Nemat and his family that I've been able to gather the information I've turned over to you."

Dempsey nodded slowly, still obviously skeptical. "My superiors are nervous."

"I'm sure they are, but they also want the information I have. Nemat is no terrorist," Carter said with emphasis.

Dempsey studied them both for a long while. "Why are you doing this for him?"

Carter reached to Nemat and took his hand. "I care for him a great deal. We intend to return to New York. Nemat is very good with cars, so we hope he can get a job doing auto repair. As you heard, he speaks very good English. We aren't asking that anyone support him, just give him a chance. He put himself in danger for the information you have and want. I think that alone proves he isn't a terrorist or threat to anyone, except maybe the government he's been fighting against."

"You're really ready to stick your neck out for him?" Dempsey asked.

"He stuck his out for me," Carter countered.

"Very well." Agent Dempsey stood up slowly. "I'll see what I can do." Carter knew he'd won. Dempsey wanted the information he had very badly.

"You know how to get in touch with me once you have your answer," Carter said. Dempsey left the room, and Carter turned to Nemat. "Get your things together. We're going to get my equipment, and then I need to get to work."

"What's the hurry?" Nemat asked.

"I need to get my story written, and as soon as Dempsey calls with his agreement, we need to be ready to move." Carter started packing his few things. "As soon as I hand over the information they want, they'll declare it classified and a matter of national security. So I need to get my story written and off to my editor before they can do that. Then I won't be in violation of any laws and we can get you in the country." Carter's heart beat a mile a minute, blood coursing through his veins. Very few things felt as good as a fantastic story. He paused and kissed Nemat hard. That was most definitely one of those things.

They left the hotel a few minutes later. Carter called Olivier, and he agreed to meet them with Carter's computer and the belongings Carter had left with him. Carter wasn't sure if they were being followed and he really didn't care.

"On a deadline, I see," Olivier said when Carter hurried up to his table at the café.

"Yes," Carter said.

"I won't keep you, then," Olivier said and handed Carter his computer bag. Carter checked it quickly and hurried back to the waiting taxi. Then he had the driver take them to a hotel. He didn't feel comfortable in a hotel arranged by the CIA. He'd suddenly thought of listening devices or cameras and smiled at the thought of them possibly getting on eyeful or earful earlier. They checked in, and Carter got right to work as soon as the room door was locked. The story he wanted to tell had been writing itself in his brain for two days. He booted up his computer and got to work. Nemat settled on the bed, and every few minutes Carter glanced at him before returning to his work. He described the empty village, the dead dog, and the shell casings, as well as the way the village had been destroyed and the narrow escape. It was a great story, and once he was done, he sent it, along with pictures of the casings and the village, to his editor. A few seconds later, he received an automated reply that his e-mail had been delivered. Then he sat on the bed next to Nemat and called his editor.

"Kent, I did it," he said when his editor answered the phone. "I just sent you the story."

"Good," Kent responded. Carter knew he was signing in to work to get his e-mail. "Jesus," Kent said after a minute or two. "Are you sure? They're just casings."

"I got them tested by someone quite reliable," Carter said with a half-smile.

Kent hesitated. "How?"

"Our friendly neighborhood spy," Carter answered. "He wants something I have, and I need something from him."

"I think you better start at the beginning and tell me everything," Kent said. "No, wait. I think you need to get out of there, come back here, and tell me in person. We'll get you booked on a flight."

"Give me a little more time," Carter said, "and I promise I'll tell you everything, even the stuff you don't want to know." He was playing with fire from both ends, and he knew it. But the risks were worth it if it meant he would be able to end up with Nemat in his life.

"Okay. But I want the next story soon." Kent disconnected, and Carter put the phone down. For the next hour or so, he waited nervously, willing his phone to ring. He and Nemat got something to eat, made a stop at an apothecary, and then returned to the room. Carter had just figured they might as well go to bed when his phone rang.

"You know, you were easy to follow," Dempsey said, and Carter chuckled. "They've agreed to your terms."

"Good. Since you know where we are, stop by and drop off the papers. I'll give you the location of the village. Then I'll be out of your hair. I promise." Carter heard the agent growl just before disconnecting. Carter was quickly tiring of the cloak-and-dagger stuff. They waited for Agent Dempsey, and when he arrived, the agent handed Nemat the papers he'd need, and Carter gave Dempsey the GPS coordinates. "You could probably have used satellite to locate the image, but this is the exact coordinates where we found the shells."

"You know we'll classify this information," Dempsey said.

"Story's already written and sent," Carter said. "But the coordinates weren't used, and I only gave the general location of the village." Dempsey shook Carter's hand.

"You have balls of steel," Dempsey said. "Just do me a favor. The next time you do something like this, call someone else." He turned toward the door.

"Thanks for your help," Carter said. Dempsey barely paused as he reached for the door. Once he was gone, Carter called Kent and asked him to make plane reservations for two. "I promise I'll explain, and it will be worth your while." He gave Kent Nemat's information for the reservation.

"It better," Kent told him. "It fucking better, or you'll find yourself bouncing down the sidewalk on your backside."

"I love you too, Kent, and you'll have the next story soon."

"See that I do," Kent said before disconnecting the call.

About half an hour later, Carter got an e-mail with their travel information. Carter sent a reply and shut down his computer after noting the time they were to leave. Then he turned to Nemat, who was resting on the bed.

"We have a flight tomorrow morning for New York," he said as he moved closer. "Are you sure you're ready?"

"Yes," Nemat answered confidently. He turned, and before Carter could react, Nemat pounced and pressed him back on the bed, a huge smile on his face. "I think I'm ready to spend some time without the sound of guns and bombs."

"You know things will be very different, and there will be a number of things you'll find frustrating and strange. New York is a huge city."

"So is Aleppo," Nemat said. "Or it was."

Carter shook his head slowly. "New York is much larger, with buildings a thousand feet tall, cars, buses, trains, people, all of it moving fast." Nemat looked as though he didn't believe him. "I'm serious. It's very different. But I'll be there for you. You won't be alone," Carter said reassuringly. Nemat still didn't seem convinced. "You'll understand when you get there."

Nemat nodded. "Okay."

Carter knew Nemat simply had to see it to believe it. "I promise I'll be there as long as you want me to be." He swallowed.

"Are you afraid?" Nemat asked him.

"Yes," Carter answered honestly. "I'm afraid you're going to come home with me and find that there's a life outside what you know now. There will be so many things open to you. What if you don't need me anymore? I had a friend, Larkin, who went away for college. He met his boyfriend, Claude, and they were happy for three years. Once they graduated, they moved to the city. While they were in college, everything was perfect. Once they came to the city, Claude changed. At first, he and Larkin went to the clubs together. Then Claude started going on his own without Larkin. After that, they only stayed together a few months. I'm not saying that will happen, but there's so much available and you should experience it."

Nemat moved closer. "Then we will experience it together."

Carter knew he wasn't going to make Nemat understand, and this wasn't Nemat's issue. It was his. He'd have to be prepared emotionally for whatever happened. There was nothing Nemat could do to reassure him, and there were no guarantees.

Nemat stroked his cheek, and Carter realized he'd been staring blankly at the wall. He turned toward Nemat, who shifted closer and kissed him. The kiss sent a shock down his back. Up until now, it had been Carter who was worldlier, who had tried to comfort and support Nemat. Now it was Nemat who deepened the kiss and pulled him closer, Nemat who slipped his hand beneath Carter's shirt and lightly stroked his skin. "Sometimes you worry too much," Nemat told him. "The world will present us all with enough worries. There's no need to add more on our own."

Carter gazed into Nemat's eyes. "Is that how you survived?"

"Maybe. I don't know. I only know that bad things happen. If you had told me when we first met that I would be here with you, I would have thought you were crazy." Nemat paused. "I'm scared too. I might never see my family again, and I'm going to a strange place. What if you are not the man I think you are? For some things, you have to have faith." Carter swallowed hard. "And I have faith in you."

Questions formed in Carter's mind, but they flew away like a bird on the wing when Nemat kissed him again. The worries were still there, but they didn't matter nearly as much. Nemat was here with him, and he was going to New York with him. Everything else could wait. Carter returned Nemat's kiss and heard him whimper softly. "I want you, Nemat," Carter whispered between kisses.

Nemat stopped still. "I don't understand."

"I'll show you," Carter said. He kissed Nemat again, pressing him back on the bed. Clothing ended up on the floor, and Carter maneuvered Nemat on top of him. "I need the bag from the store," he whispered as he stretched, shifting the grab the bag. He reached in and pulled out a small tube of slick. It wasn't what he would normally use, but it would work. He handed it to Nemat. "Use some on your fingers."

Nemat's eyes went wide and then he nodded. Carter watched him open the tube and squirt a dollop of gel onto his fingers. "Are you sure?" Nemat asked.

"Yes," Carter answered. Nemat gently probed Carter's opening and then slowly worked a finger inside him. Carter groaned, and Nemat stilled. "It's good," he hissed softly.

Nemat was a natural. Once he realized he wasn't hurting Carter, he began moving and then added a second finger. Carter then moaned. Nemat quickly realized what Carter liked and was soon driving him crazy. Whenever Carter caught his breath, Nemat scissored, or bent his finger, and sent Carter flying once again. When Nemat pulled his fingers away, Carter groaned. It took him a few seconds to realize Nemat was watching him. Through his lust-addled brain, Carter found his wallet and handed Nemat the single condom he had.

Nemat stared at it. Carter opened the package and rolled the condom down Nemat's length, loving the way Nemat's eyes rolled at the sensation. He loved that his touch could make Nemat respond like that, and he vibrated with energy. Carter lubed the condom, then guided Nemat into position and encouraged him to press forward.

Carter's breath flew from his lungs as Nemat breached him for the first time. Nemat gasped and stopped, locking gazes with him. Carter patted his hip to encourage him to move. He pressed forward, filling Carter more and more. Carter arched his back and pushed as best he could, sliding Nemat deeper.

He wanted release, desperately. From deep inside, his instinct was to take control, but Carter tamped it down. He needed Nemat to be able to have control. Each of Nemat's touches was so gentle and soft… careful. Carter usually wanted more of a firm touch, but every time Nemat moved, Carter saw stars. He'd waited so very long to be connected to Nemat that he could hardly believe it was happening. Nemat pressed his hips to Carter's butt.

Carter swore under his breath, willing his muscles to relax. He could feel Nemat's energy and knew his instinct was to thrust. When Nemat began to move, Carter moaned and swallowed hard. Nemat was thick, and the burn lasted a long time. He pulled Nemat forward, kissing him deeply. He needed as much contact as he could get. Nemat slowly began to move his hips. Carter dang near bit Nemat's lips as the sensation hit him. He opened his mouth, sucking air from out of Nemat's mouth.

Nemat's tiny movements continued, his cock jumping inside Carter, driving him crazy. Carter had never experienced anything like this. Sex was usually hard and fast, but Nemat was slow, patient, and then Carter realized this wasn't just sex for him—this was making love. What hit him harder was that it was making love for Nemat as well. The warmth in his eyes, the gentleness of the touch, all of it communicated clearly how Nemat felt. Carter's heart jumped at the realization, and his passion skyrocketed. He had never felt this way before. "Nemat," Carter whimpered.

"I'm loving you," Nemat whispered, his lips right near Carter's. "I love you for always."

"I love you too," Carter said. It was amazing to him how alive Nemat seemed. It was probably his imagination, but the energy and vitality in Nemat seemed different. He wanted to ask, but Nemat picked up his pace, snapping his hips, and Carter forgot about such unimportant things. All that mattered was Nemat and him. The world outside their hotel room, even just beyond the bed, didn't mean a thing. All that Carter cared about was him, right here and now. "I think I've loved you for a long time, but was too stubborn to tell you."

Nemat snapped his hips harder. Carter groaned and gritted his teeth as pulses of ecstasy shot through him. "You will always tell me now." He snapped his hips again, making Carter's cock bounce on his belly.

"Whatever you want," Carter said. "Just don't stop. No matter what, don't stop."

Nemat thrust faster. "I'll never stop. You can always tell me things, and I will never stop." He encircled Carter's cock with his long fingers and slowly stroked him. Damn, that felt good.

Soon Carter could hardly see. He focused his attention strictly on Nemat's touch and the way he made him feel. Nothing else existed. Carter wondered how long he could last. His entire body was already tingling. He could barely feel his feet, and his head throbbed with thinly controlled excitement. Carter's mouth hung open, and he constantly licked his lips to keep them from going as dry as his mouth felt. "More... just... more."

Nemat maintained a steady pace. Carter continued begging as he balanced on the razor's edge of unbelievable pleasure. Nemat stroked just a little faster, but not enough to push Carter over the edge. Carter whined and then growled, trying to get Nemat to send him what he needed. He didn't. Carter held there for what seemed like forever. He listened as Nemat's breathing became ragged and the thrusting less rhythmic. Carter clamped his eyes shut, focusing only on the pleasure.

Nemat thrust hard and deep. Carter groaned and gasped as he felt Nemat throb deep inside him and then still. He needed just a little bit more; he was right there, and yet he balanced like a tightrope walker in a gale, ready to tumble at any second. He held there until Nemat tightened his grip and stroked him faster and faster. Lights flashed behind Carter's eyes, and he stilled as he came with mind-blowing force.

Carter couldn't move. He didn't want to. Everything should stay just the way it was for a long time. He was floating on happy thoughts with Nemat holding him. Slowly he came back down to earth. He realized he and Nemat were still connected, and it felt damned good. He whimpered when their bodies disconnected and waited while Nemat took care of the condom.

Carter heard Nemat in the bathroom, and then he returned with a cloth. Nemat cleaned him up and hurried away once more. When he returned a few seconds later, Nemat pulled down the covers, and they climbed beneath them in the air-conditioned room. "It's cold," Nemat told him. "I haven't been in air conditioning in a long time."

Carter curled up next to him and turned out the light. He was asleep within minutes, holding Nemat, just the way he'd dreamed of.

THEY WOKE in the morning, and packed their things. Their flight didn't leave until the afternoon, so they stopped at a shopping center and got Nemat some clothes and a small bag before taking a taxi to the airport. Carter called Olivier while they were en route and thanked him for all his help.

They checked in, showed their identification, and made their way through security. At their gate, they sat and waited for their flight to be called. When it was their turn, he and Nemat boarded the plane and sat next to each other in the business-class section. Nemat sat nervously as the other passengers boarded. Then the doors were closed, announcements were made, and the plane began to move.

"It's okay," Carter said, leaning close to Nemat.

"I know. I'm with you." Nemat flashed him a quick smile as the plane turned and then picked up speed. Faster and faster they went, until the jumbo jet lifted off the ground and climbed into the sky. They were on their way home, Carter back to where he lived and Nemat to a new home. Carter knew that for both of them, life would be very different from now on, but they were both heading to their home and a new life. Carter reached over the armrest and took Nemat's hand. Nemat interlaced their fingers as the plane tilted slightly, changing directions, heading west. The life they would begin together was just a few hours away.

EPILOGUE

One year later

CARTER HURRIED home from work. Nemat would have gotten home a half hour earlier, and Carter expected him to be a nervous wreck. He kicked the slush off his shoes and hurried up the stairs—they were faster than waiting for the elevator—to the larger fifth-floor apartment they'd rented together, and the door opened. His old apartment had been fine, but hadn't offered enough space for them longer term.

"We're going to be late," Nemat told him impatiently but with a slight smile that made Carter's heart thump.

"I know, I'm sorry," Carter said. "I told them I had to get out early, but there was a crisis and I ended up dashing off my thoughts for one of the other reporters." Carter slipped his bag off his shoulder and leaned in for a kiss that heated quickly. His bag hit the floor with a soft thunk, and he hugged Nemat tighter.

"Carter," Nemat whispered. "The car will be here in five minutes." Nervous energy flowed off Nemat. Carter stroked his cheek and then picked up his bag and hurried inside. He dropped the bag on the sofa without breaking stride toward the bedroom, already removing his shirt. Nemat had laid fresh clothes out for him on the bed. Carter stripped and dressed himself without thinking.

Nemat had discovered a love of fashion Carter had never expected. He had become enthralled with the way people dressed almost as soon as they had landed after the long trip from Turkey. Their initial shopping expedition for Nemat's wardrobe had quickly shifted from a simple trip to Macy's into an entirely new way of looking at things for Nemat. They spent days together looking at what was in style. Nemat was a very careful shopper, but he quickly developed his own colorful sense of style, one that seemed to be rubbing off on Carter. His wardrobe had gone from bland to bold.

As Carter finished dressing, he let his eyes drift over the photographs on the bedroom walls. There had been difficult times for Nemat. Nearly everything, from acquiring a taste for the food, to the proximity of neighbors, to the sounds of the city, had been completely new and different for Nemat. There had been times when he'd told Carter he'd hated New York and that he craved something, anything, that felt like home. They went to the park a lot, but that didn't really help much either, because everything looked different. At first, Carter hadn't known what to do, but then he remembered the photographs he'd taken with his phone. Carter sent them to one of the ultratalented people at the paper's photographic department, and she cleaned up the hastily taken images and had them printed on quality photographic stock. Now there were photographs of Nemat's family on the walls in the bedroom, and in the living room were the pictures of the olive grove and buildings in the compound. Carter had even found a picture from his first visit to the house, before it had been destroyed. In the bathroom, small pictures of the spring and creek hung on the walls. As Carter pulled on his shoes, a lump formed in his throat as he remembered how tears had welled in Nemat's eyes when he'd given him the framed photographs.

"Are you ready?" Nemat asked from the bedroom doorway and tossed Carter his winter coat, his own already on and an extra coat draped over his arm.

"Yes." Carter stood up and followed Nemat as he practically ran out of the apartment. Carter locked the door and met Nemat on the sidewalk as a car pulled up in front of them. Nemat got in the backseat, and Carter followed him and pulled the door closed.

"I hope we're not late," Nemat said.

"He won't be alone," Carter told him, taking Nemat's hand. Nemat had been a nervous wreck for the last three days, ever since they'd gotten the call from the aid agency that Jalal would be arriving to join his brother. At first, Nemat had been thrilled, but over the past few days, a million questions had surfaced for Nemat, and with each one, his nerves had increased. The civil war in Syria had ground on over that period, with each side making little long-term headway. But the back and forth in the conflict was slowly destroying what was left of the country.

"I know. The refugee agency promised there would be someone with him," Nemat said, barely able to sit still on the seat.

They rode out of Manhattan, across the river to Queens, and out to LaGuardia. The driver handed Carter a card. "Call when you're ready to go back, and I'll bring the car around."

"Thank you," Carter said and then turned to catch up with Nemat, who was already hurrying inside. He reached him as Nemat stood in front of the flight board. "They landed a few minutes ago." Carter gently patted Nemat's hand. "Let's go to the waiting area. It will probably be half an hour or so."

"Okay," Nemat whispered. They walked to the passenger-receiving area of the international terminal and stared as people came down the escalator, watching for Jalal. Carter knew something pretty bad must have happened if Jalal was coming alone. Carter tried not to concentrate on that and to simply be there for Nemat. His own worries and concerns were secondary. Nemat's agitation grew by the second and then he gasped. Carter saw Jalal at almost the exact same time. He was painfully thin, leaning on crutches—his left foot and lower leg were gone.

Nemat sniffed and stepped forward, letting Jalal step off the escalator and out of the flow of traffic before hugging him tightly. Neither said a word, but Carter saw tears run down Nemat's cheek as they continued holding each other.

When they separated, Nemat stepped back, and Carter walked forward, greeting Jalal with a careful hug and then a handshake. "Do you have luggage?"

Jalal stared at Carter for a few seconds and then shook his head. "It's just me."

"Then let's get you back to the apartment and settled," Carter said. He wasn't sure what he was supposed to do at this point and let

Nemat take the lead. They'd gotten a call three days earlier from the Red Cross explaining that Jalal had gotten out of the country. The Red Cross contact had explained that they could get him into the US because he'd be persecuted for political reasons if he returned to Syria.

They left the airport, moving slowly. Nemat stopped them at the door and handed Jalal the extra coat he'd brought for him. Winter weather was another thing that had taken Nemat a long time to get used to. Carter called for the car, and the driver pulled around about five minutes later. Carter got in, and Nemat helped Jalal into the backseat.

As they rode the forty minutes to the city, Nemat and Jalal talked quietly. Carter heard Nemat gasp more than once, and his fears were confirmed. The compound had been attacked again, and this time the only survivor had been Jalal. He didn't speak about losing his leg, but Carter could put the pieces together.

"I'm not whole," Carter heard Jalal say in Arabic. He and Nemat had continued working together to both improve Nemat's English and Carter's Arabic. He was pretty proficient now.

"Yes, you are. And you're here now, with us," Nemat said. Carter brought down the visor and used the mirror to glance at Jalal. The expression on his face told him that at the very least he suspected the nature of his and Nemat's relationship. When they'd received the call and knew Jalal was coming, he and Nemat had talked about what to tell him and had agreed they weren't going to hide.

Jalal grew quiet, and Carter sighed. This was going to be more difficult than he'd hoped. Eventually, Jalal spoke with Nemat, but his tone was clipped and definitely hostile.

The driver pulled up in front of their apartment building, and they got out. Nemat helped Jalal to the elevator, and Carter used the stairs. He'd already gotten the door unlocked by the time the elevator doors slid open. Nemat helped Jalal into the apartment and got him settled on the sofa. Jalal looked around the room, and Carter saw his gaze fall on the framed pictures of what had once been his home. "Where did you get these?" he asked Nemat, who answered rapidly.

Their conversation shifted from there with Jalal firing questions at Nemat.

"Jalal," Carter snapped, bringing the mini inquisition to a halt momentarily.

"I not talk to you," Jalal said in English.

"That's enough," Carter told him. "You need to listen."

"No, Carter, I'll explain it to him," Nemat said. Carter nodded. He thought about leaving the room, but wasn't sure how Jalal would act toward Nemat, and there was no way he would let anything happen to him. "Things are different here, Jalal," Nemat said firmly. "I have learned a lot about myself and who I am. Things I've always known, but could never talk about. Loving Carter has allowed me to be happy and to be the person I'm meant to be."

"But it is wrong," Jalal said accusingly.

Nemat sat next to his brother. "I know this is hard for you, but do you remember when we were in Canada with Mama and Papa? He always told us that different people lived different lives. Well, my life is different, and you can either accept that or not. But this is our home— Carter's and mine."

Jalal simply nodded and was quiet for a while. "Were you like this before you left?"

"Yes. I've always been like this." Nemat sat next to Jalal. "I love him. This isn't something dirty or shameful. We care for each other the way Mama and Papa cared for each other."

For a second, Carter saw anger rise in Jalal's eyes, but it faded just as quickly. "What do I know? The things I held dear are all gone." Jalal swallowed.

"We are family, Jalal. I know this is hard for you, but you will come to understand. Here everything is different. People are different, and they believe things that are not the same as back home."

"Home is gone, Nemat," Jalal said.

"I know. What we had there is gone, but this is our home now."

"How can I live here?" Jalal asked. "What will people think?"

"That you have family that cares for you," Nemat said and then stood up. "You do what you think best, but it isn't going to change the way we feel or the fact that this is our home. We are willing to open our lives and share them with you because we're family. We're all we have left." Carter heard the hitch in Nemat's voice, and nothing could keep him away any longer. He went to stand next to Nemat and gently touched his shoulder.

"He's going to need some time," Carter said softly and then looked to Jalal. "I want you to think about something. Your brother is still the same person he always was. He took care of the family in your absence. He looked after them as you would have. He fought alongside you and watched your back just like you did his. Who he loves doesn't make him any less a man or any less your brother."

"But all we were taught—" Jalal said feebly.

"What's important is family taking care of family," Carter said. "Just think about it." Carter turned to Jalal. "We made up a room for you." It had been his office, but they'd quickly refurnished it for Jalal once they'd known he was coming. "Nemat will show you." Jalal used the crutches to stand, and Nemat showed him to the second bedroom. The two of them disappeared inside and closed the door. Carter listened outside for a few seconds, expecting yelling, but when he heard only whispers, he went into the kitchen to start dinner.

As he worked, Carter kept one eye on the door. He wasn't sure what he expected, but he nearly cut himself twice, paying more attention to what might be happening than what he was doing. Eventually, Carter put everything away to save his fingers. They could go out for dinner.

After about an hour, the door opened and Nemat walked out. His eyes were puffy and red. He closed the door behind him. "Jalal is sleeping," Nemat told him.

"Is everything okay?" Carter asked, knowing it really wasn't.

"It will be," Nemat told him with a forced smile that quickly faded. "He confirmed that everyone else is gone. They were killed in an attack. Jalal wasn't even sure who attacked them. He was injured, but managed to find some help." He sniffed. "But not in time to save his leg." Carter was around the kitchen worktable in a flash, pulling

Nemat to him, gently stroking his hair as he held Nemat close. There was nothing he could do except be there for whatever Nemat needed, and he intended to be. Images of their time together in Syria flashed in his memory—hard times when he'd wanted to comfort Nemat but couldn't. Now he could and did without hesitation or second thought.

They stood together. Carter held Nemat, feeling the grief and loss wash through the man he loved more than anyone in the world. Tears welled in his own eyes for Nemat's family and the loss of so many people he'd come to know. "We could go for a walk. Will he be okay for a while?" Carter asked, glancing toward the room Jalal was using. He expected to see a closed door, but Jalal stood in the doorway, watching them.

He braced himself for rage and yelling, but Jalal didn't even scowl. He simply watched them for a few seconds, nodded once when their eyes met, and quietly closed the door. Carter closed his eyes and held Nemat tighter.

"I love you, and I'll be here no matter what," Carter whispered. Nemat tilted his head upward, and Carter kissed him. The February wind whistled outside the windows as the light began to fade. But Carter knew spring would come and things would get better. Grief would pass, and in the end Nemat and Jalal would be a family again. It would take time, but he knew in his heart it would happen. "It'll be okay."

Nemat nestled closer. "I know," he whispered. "I have everything I really need, because I have you." Nemat sniffed slightly, met Carter's gaze, and then kissed him.

ANDREW GREY grew up in western Michigan with a father who loved to tell stories and a mother who loved to read them. Since then he has lived all over the country and traveled throughout the world. He has a master's degree from the University of Wisconsin-Milwaukee and works in information systems for a large corporation. Andrew's hobbies include collecting antiques, gardening, and leaving his dirty dishes anywhere but in the sink (particularly when writing). He considers himself blessed with an accepting family, fantastic friends, and the world's most supportive and loving partner. Andrew currently lives in beautiful historic Carlisle, Pennsylvania.

Visit Andrew's website at http://www.andrewgreybooks.com and blog at http://andrewgreybooks.livejournal.com/.

E-mail him at andrewgrey@comcast.net.

The Art Series from ANDREW GREY

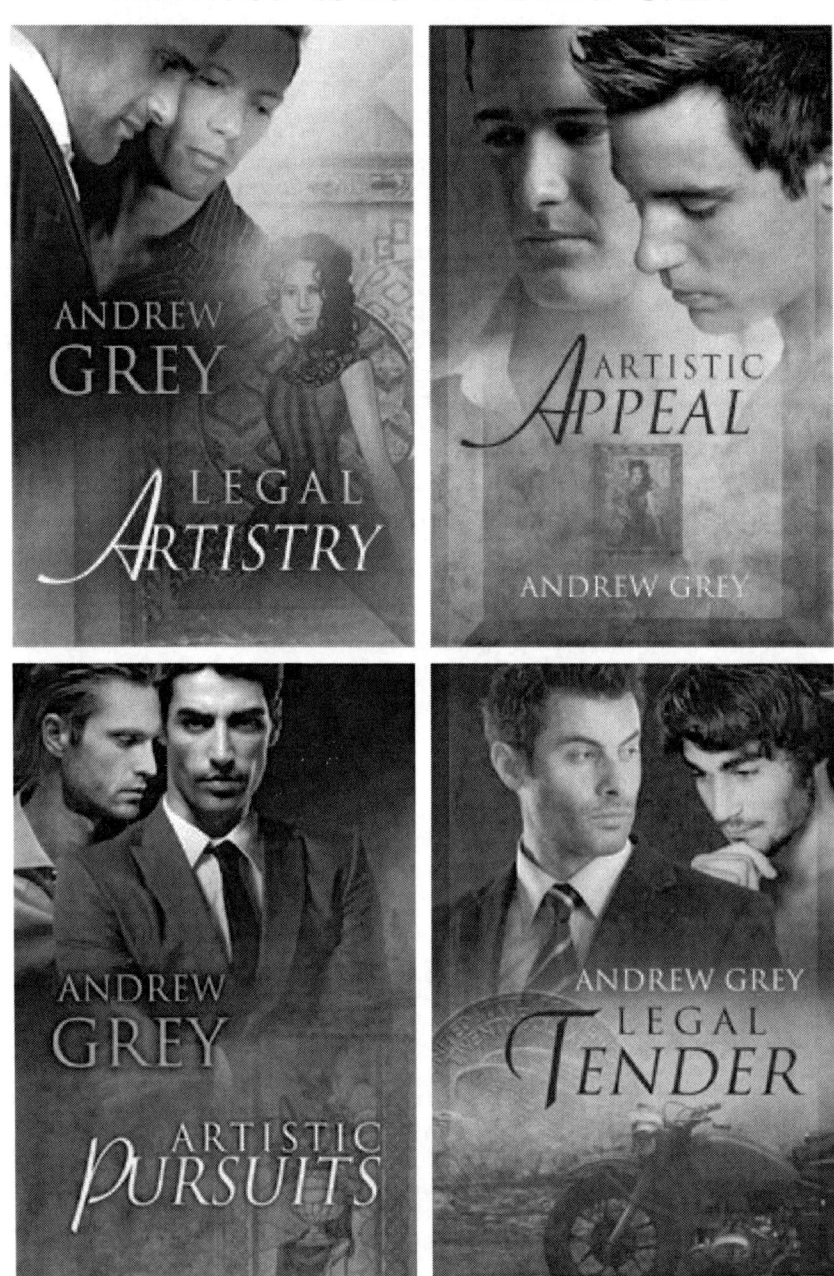

http://www.dreamspinnerpress.com

The Bottled Up Series from ANDREW GREY

http://www.dreamspinnerpress.com

Love Means… Series from ANDREW GREY

Love Means… Series from ANDREW GREY

http://www.dreamspinnerpress.com

Taste of Love Stories from ANDREW GREY

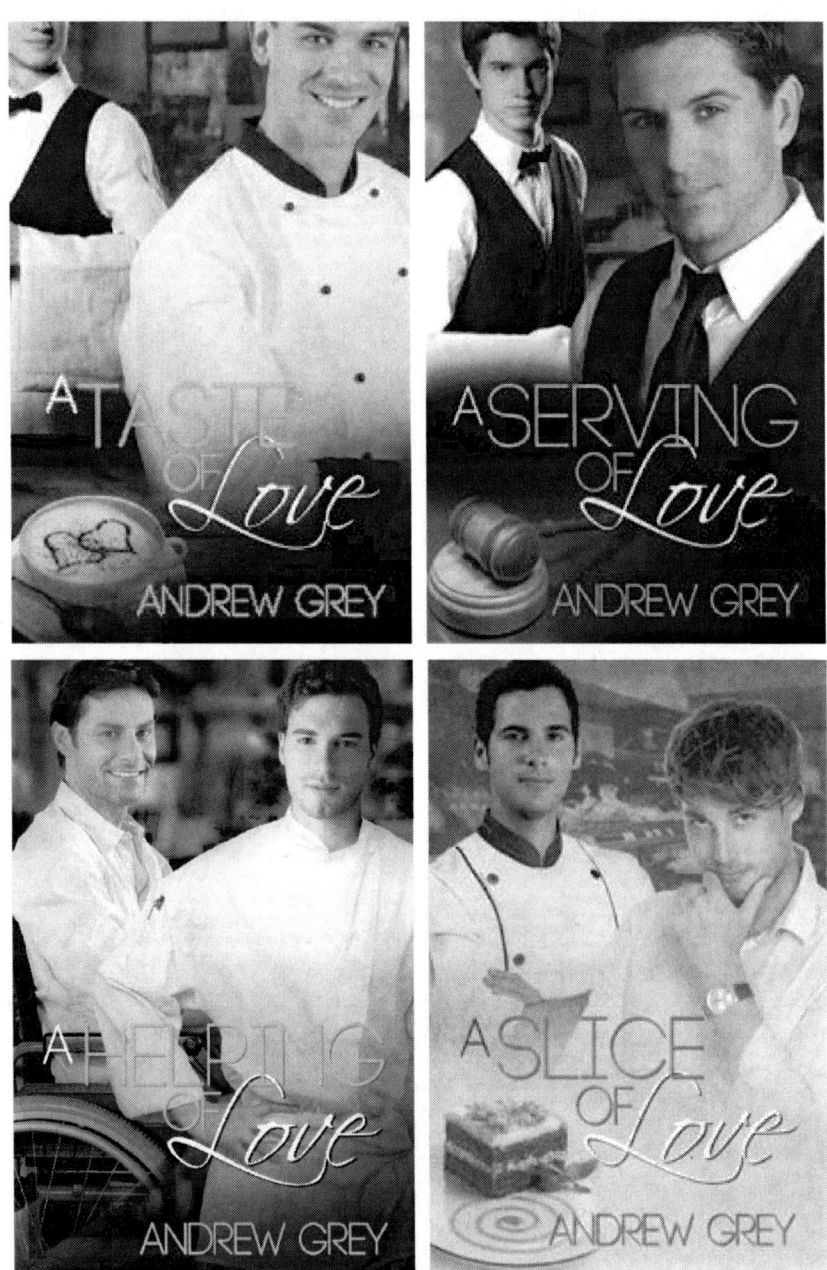

http://www.dreamspinnerpress.com

Children of Bacchus Stories from ANDREW GREY

http://www.dreamspinnerpress.com

Good Fight Stories from ANDREW GREY

http://www.dreamspinnerpress.com

Stories from the Range from ANDREW GREY

http://www.dreamspinnerpress.com

Stories from the Range from ANDREW GREY

The Bullriders from ANDREW GREY

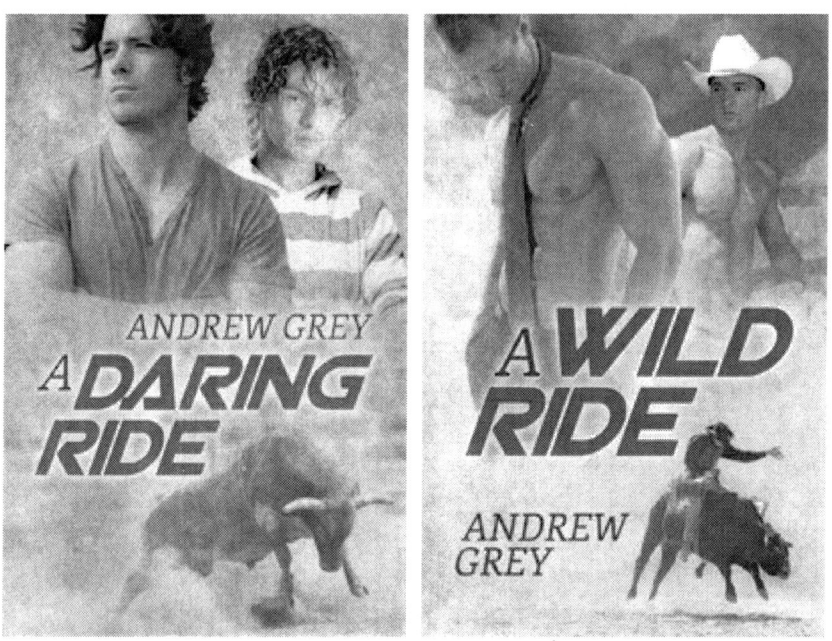

http://www.dreamspinnerpress.com

Senses Stories from A<small>NDREW</small> G<small>REY</small>

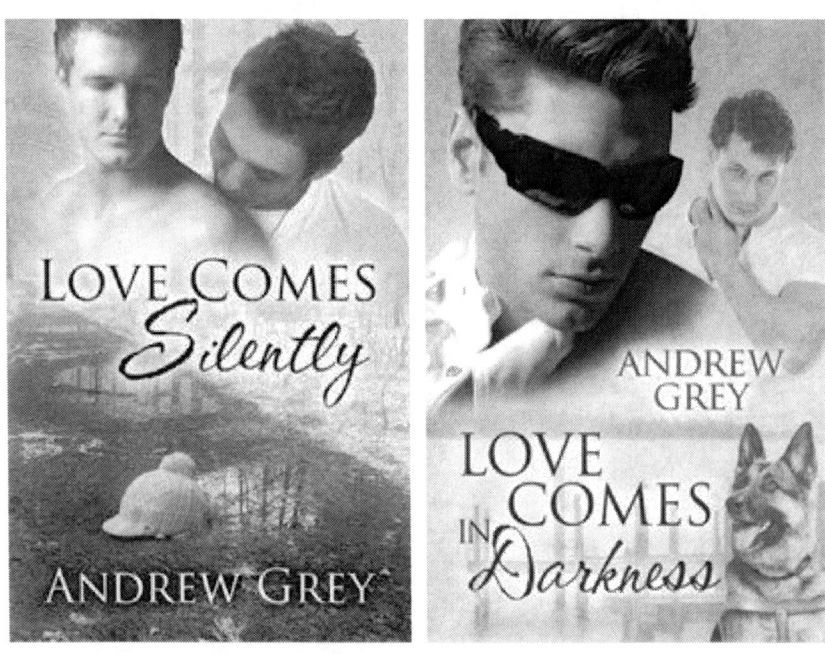

http://www.dreamspinnerpress.com

Seven Days Stories from ANDREW GREY

http://www.dreamspinnerpress.com

The Fire Series from ANDREW GREY

http://www.dreamspinnerpress.com

Work Out Series from ANDREW GREY

http://www.dreamspinnerpress.com

Work Out Series from ANDREW GREY

http://www.dreamspinnerpress.com

Children of Bacchus Stories from ANDREW GREY

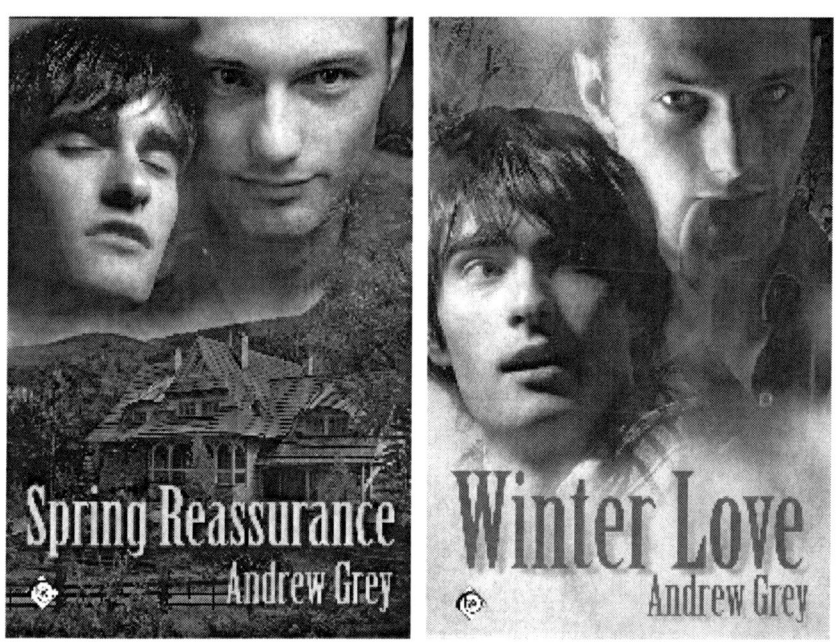

http://www.dreamspinnerpress.com

Also from ANDREW GREY

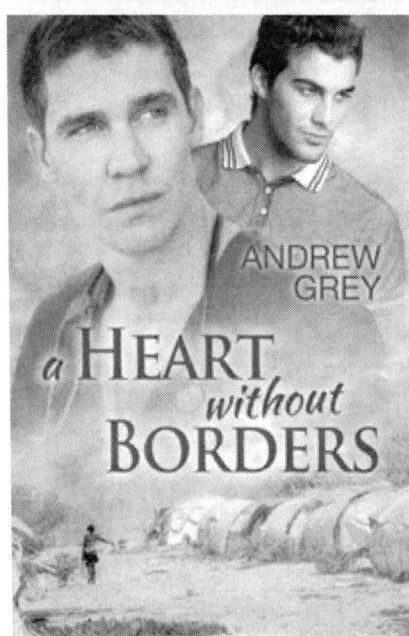
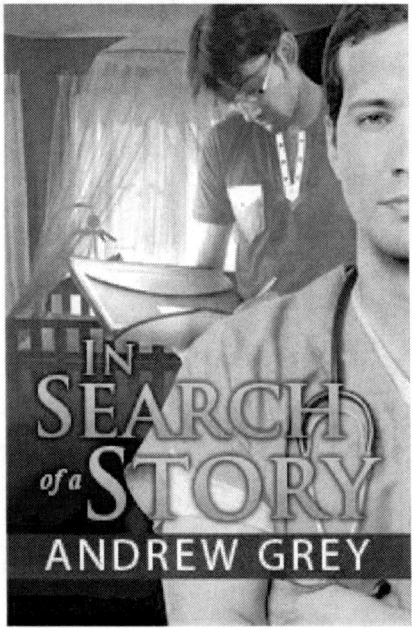

http://www.dreamspinnerpress.com

Also from ANDREW GREY

http://www.dreamspinnerpress.com

Novellas from ANDREW GREY

Novellas from ANDREW GREY

CPSIA information can be obtained at www.ICGtesting.com
Printed in the USA
LVOW12s0426120614

389570LV00003B/201/P